a4

"But do you agree? No more?"

Kim spread her hands, feeling melodramatic making such a fuss about a mere kiss. Except that to her it wasn't a mere kiss, but a key to heaven or hell.

"No more kisses? No more touching? No more red roses? What sort of life do you want, Kim?" Con's voice had roughened, and he covered the distance between them quickly, taking her savagely into his arms, all humor having fled. "Are you trying to drive me out of my mind? Can't you see how I feel about you? And you want me, Kim, don't deny it. You're as crazy for me as I am for you."

Flames of desire seemed to leap between them. Somehow she managed to croak, "I don't want you—you're the man who killed my mother!"

SALLY HEYWOOD is a British author, born in Yorkshire. After leaving university, she had several jobs, including running an art gallery, a guest house and a boutique. She has written several plays for theater and television, as well as novels for the Harlequin romance series. Her special interests are sailing, reading, fashion, interior decorating and helping in a children's nursery.

Books by Sally Heywood

HARLEQUIN PRESENTS
1200—FANTASY LOVER
1235—TODAY, TOMORROW, AND FOREVER

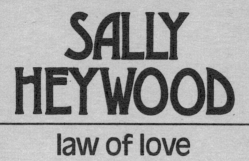

SALLY HEYWOOD

law of love

Harlequin Books

TORONTO • NEW YORK • LONDON
AMSTERDAM • PARIS • SYDNEY • HAMBURG
STOCKHOLM • ATHENS • TOKYO • MILAN

Harlequin Presents first edition April 1990
ISBN 0-373-11256-4

Original hardcover edition published in 1989
by Mills & Boon Limited

CHAPTER ONE

THE MAN tore along the corridor, black gown streaming out behind him as he advanced towards her. He was in quite a hurry. Kim prepared to step back out of the way rather than risk being sent flying, but as he drew near she saw him hesitate. In the ill-lit corridor behind the Law Courts it was difficult to make much out, but even so, she too faltered. That strong, dark, good-looking face seemed unexpectedly familiar.

He obviously recognised her too, as soon as he came within range. A smile broke over the clean-cut features, dazzling her, turning her knees to jelly. 'What are *you* doing here?' He skidded to a stop just in front of her. 'Not in trouble, I hope?'

'I'm not, but my company is, and I'm here to give moral support,' she told him, lifting her head. She hadn't realised he was so tall.

He shifted the sheaf of papers under one arm and hesitated. 'I can't stop—I'm due in court.' He snatched a glance at his watch and grimaced. 'Five minutes ago, actually. But later, if you're going to be around——?' he shrugged. 'Look, I've got to go. What's the case?' He was halfway along the corridor already.

'Image Design versus Jackpot Photographic.'

He pulled a face. 'You're nothing to do with Jackpot, are you?'

Kim shook her head. 'The other side.'

'Thank heavens for that!' He gave a boyish grin, then took another glance at his watch. 'I've just been having a word with your boss, Ian Robertson. He'll put you in the picture.' He touched her on the arm. 'We definitely will meet afterwards. See you in court!'

With that he hurried off down the corridor and she watched him push open a panelled door further down. It closed firmly behind him.

'Boss?' she mused as she turned towards the public gallery. 'Partner, please, Mr X!' It didn't rankle as much as it usually did. She was always being mistaken for Ian's secretary. Just because she was twenty-two and looked—well, frankly, she admitted it herself, no more than seventeen! What this heavenly-looking man had to do with the case she didn't know, but at least he wasn't working for the opposition—judging by the delicious smile when she told him she was nothing to do with Jackpot!

Confused by the meeting, she pushed everything to one side as she went into the courtroom and took her seat beside Ian and Laura.

'I've just been mistaken for you again,' whispered Kim as she slipped in beside Laura. It was a standing joke, sometimes turned to their advantage with particular clients, the sort who'll say what they really think about a piece of artwork to a secretary but are rather less forthcoming to the artist.

Laura put her hand on Kim's arm. 'You've missed all the excitement. Ian nearly hit the roof a few minutes ago when they told him our barrister chap had laryngitis. But we've got someone else from the same group.'

'Set,' corrected Kim. 'And that explains something—I'll tell you later.' Her eyes scanned the tables down at the front beneath the judge's dais. Yes, there he was now, black gown draped untidily over broad shoulders and on his head a short white wig, for goodness' sake! Instead of detracting from the handsome, rather arrogant lines of his face it actually seemed to add something, a dignity, a rather scary authority.

As if reading Kim's thoughts Laura followed her glance, then turned to her. 'I see you've noticed that gorgeous brute on the left. Guess who he belongs to.'

'What?' Kim's heart gave an unexpected lurch.

'What's wrong? You don't know him, do you?'

Kim ignored this. 'What do you mean, belongs to? Is he married?'

'Probably. But I didn't mean that. I mean he belongs to *us*. He's the fill-in for old Maxwell. Aren't we the lucky ones? I hope the case goes on for years and years!'

Kim felt a wave of relief scudding up her body. It was irrational, but she didn't want the man down there to be married. Just then the usher called for the court to stand and a judge, swathed in red, came shuffling through a door at the back, climbed laboriously on to his dais and, with much pulling and rearranging of his robes, eventually sat down and the hearing proceeded.

Through the ensuing formalities Kim couldn't help letting her mind wander. She didn't know the name of what Laura called 'their man', but by the time a break was called an hour and a half later she felt she knew every nuance of his expression, every line in the strongly etched features as he argued their case.

'Let's go and have a coffee. There's a place round the corner.' Ian ushered them both out under the echoing dome of the court foyer and Laura jigged from foot to foot, pleased to be able to stretch her legs.

'At last we can talk in our normal voices. What is it about these places that makes one whisper? Well, Kim,' she clutched her arm excitedly, 'what do you think?' She gave her a nudge, shooting a sidelong glance at Ian as she did so.

'I don't know what you mean!' laughed Kim, heading towards the doors. 'Let's have that drink. I'm still spooked by law courts. Things seem to be going well for us, but I don't have any faith in justice as such.'

They went out into the square. It was still raining, and Kim's dark shoulder-length hair curled up into tight ringlets as the rain fell on it. By the time they reached the café it was in its usual dark tangle. 'So much for the sleek, soignée look of the successful plaintiff,' she observed, plumping down in a seat by the window and peering at her reflection in the glass. 'You are lucky, Laura, having straight hair.' She pushed the cups and saucers left by the previous customers to one end of the formica table.

'You're being quite cool about all this, Kim,' observed Ian as he sat down opposite. 'I thought you'd be freaking out at being in court.'

'Curiosity wouldn't let me stay away. I'd be on tenterhooks wondering how everything was going. And anyhow, all that legal horror was years ago.'

'You must hate the very thought of barristers.' Laura gave her a sympathetic look.

'They're only doing their job, I suppose.' Kim bit her lip. 'For a long time I did hate them. It seemed as if they were more interested in making names for themselves than doing justice, and to hell with the innocent party. But I don't know—perhaps there are some good apples!'

'Like, for instance?' Laura wagged her head from side to side and gave a teasing glance in Ian's direction. 'Don't listen to this, darling, we're drooling over our man out there. I don't suppose you noticed how dishy he is.' She turned to Kim. 'He even has a gorgeous voice, though I suppose that's part of his stock in trade.'

'He's also very good at his job.' Ian pretended to ignore Laura's remarks and addressed himself to Kim. 'Maxwell said we were lucky to get him. He's the whiz-kid of the set, a list of cases pending as long as your arm, but apparently he stitched up his last one in record time and, as he owed Maxwell a favour, he agreed to take us on. He seems to expect it to be settled tomorrow, if not before, should the other side decide to settle out of court.'

Laura pulled a face before Kim could say anything. 'What a pity. I was hoping to have the next six weeks off work to do court duty—drooling over him every day. Oh well, perhaps I'll become a professional law-breaker and hire him as my own personal lawman.'

'You are an idiot, Laura!' Kim laughed, relieved to find that neither of her two companions was interested in pursuing her traumatic experience of the law just now.

'He probably looks like nothing on earth without the wig and gown,' scoffed Ian, obviously piqued by Laura's smitten expression. They had been going through a rough patch recently. Even so, Kim couldn't help spoiling Ian's illusions.

''Fraid he's every bit as gorgeous in real life. I've actually met him already. In fact, it was last night with Lizzie. She knew how I felt about court cases and told me I needed the opposite of aversion therapy. The treatment involved meeting her law-student brother and some of his friends to convince me they were almost human, and you know how these pub evenings steamroller? We finished up in a bar near the Inns of Court . . .' She felt her voice tail away.

She was turning out to be as silly as Laura when it came to falling for complete strangers. Scarcely a day went past without Laura floating into the studio starry-eyed over some man she had glimpsed on a bus or across the street. It drove poor Ian mad. But it must be catching, for Kim had scarcely said more than hello to the man in the bar last night. He had come in with a group of people, some of whom knew Lizzie's friends, and there had been at least half a dozen chatting people sitting between them. It had all come down to what Laura would have called very heavy eye contact. But at least his impact on her hadn't been total imagination. He had remembered her face too!

She explained this to Ian and Laura. 'I'm not surprised he remembered me this morning. We were sitting opposite each other and every time I sneaked a glance at him he seemed to be just turning to look at me! I finished up not knowing where to look! I was almost glad when he got up and went out.' She paused. 'If he is married, Laura, she's a six-foot redhead in a very short tight skirt.'

Laura pursed her lips. 'So that's his type, is it? Just my luck!' She patted Ian's hand where it rested on the table. 'But you like short, chubby blondes, don't you, darling?'

He caught her hand firmly in his own. 'Don't go trying to make up to me, Laura James, just because you feel jilted.' He spoke humorously, but his grey eyes were serious.

'Jilted nothing. Kim obviously got in first!'

'Unfortunately I'm not a redhead and I'm nearer five four than six feet. Apart from that, I'm ideally suited. It's his bad luck I'm not looking!'

They all laughed. Kim let Laura and Ian's banter wash over her for the next few minutes. She suspected they were both nervous about the outcome of the case. For herself, although she made light of the morning's experience, all the old fear and long-buried anger had come rushing to the surface as soon as she had heard the judge begin to speak. It had been in a place like that in exactly those dry, measured, unemotional tones that her whole life had been transformed. She had known, even at ten and in all the years that followed, that she should forgive and forget. But later, with what happened afterwards, forgiveness was the last thing on her mind. And some things, she found, could not be forgotten.

'Come on, partner, time we went back.' Ian pulled at her arm and ushered both of them outside.

As they returned to the imposing Victorian Gothic courthouse they bumped into the two men from Jackpot Photographic. Heads were averted, and the opposing parties made their way back towards the public gallery as if they hadn't noticed each other. A prickle of apprehension ran up and down Kim's spine. Ian left her and Laura at the door. 'This is where I do my Perry Mason bit. I hope I don't fluff my lines!'

'Sock it to 'em, darling,' whispered Laura, giving his arm a squeeze before he went. 'He is sweet, isn't he?' she whispered in Kim's ear as they sat down.

'Then why are you so horrible to him?' Kim whispered back. 'If I had someone who adored me the way Ian adores you I'd be sweetness itself!'

'Only if you felt sure he was the one for you—otherwise you'd fight, like me.' Laura shivered. 'I can feel the net tightening and I'm not sure I'm ready for marriage yet! You wait until it's you, then you'll know how I feel.'

At that point the barristers came back in, and both girls turned to watch. Kim still didn't know his name. It was too late to ask Laura now because the usher was already calling for silence. Now she referred to him in her thoughts as 'our man'.

He was certainly slick. His silver tongue put Ian at ease straight away and in a few short sentences he managed to draw out all the information he needed to put their case in its best light. It wasn't a life-or-death issue. The outcome wouldn't change anybody's life. It would cost the defendants something, but no more than they deserved for stealing some of Ian's sketches and passing them off as the property of Jackpot. It was a question of copyright. Ian didn't like his own work or that of his employees being stolen by competitors and had decided to make a stand. He had discussed it thoroughly with Kim first. 'There's a slight risk. Maxwell is a friend of Dad's. He advises us to go ahead. It's a question of competition, isn't it? If we're going to survive in the jungle we're going to have to stand up and fight. He thinks it's a watertight case, but if we lost it would cost us. And at this stage of our development we need every penny we earn to survive.'

Kim had hesitated, but only for a minute or two. Anything to do with the law was hateful to her. She explained the reasons to Ian, then finished up by telling him she agreed with him. They would have to go ahead, for the sake of their business. It was no good letting the bigger company, Jackpot, push them around.

'I suppose they're scared of us. This is a small town and up till now they've been the big boys on the design and publicity scene. Now we've come in and they're doing all they can to put us out of business. Of course we fight.'

Now she was buoyed up by the grim expressions on the faces of the opposition and the good showing Ian had made under the expert questioning of his barrister. 'Our man's doing brilliantly so far,' she whispered. She crossed her fingers on her lap and gave Laura a quick smile.

By lunchtime the defendants' case was looking very shaky indeed, and Ian was cautiously jubilant as Kim and Laura met him in the entrance.

'You were wonderful, darling,' murmured Laura, going up to him and giving him a kiss as if he had just come off stage.

'Let's have a bite to eat while we wait to see if they're going to settle out of court. Come on, our chap's going to meet us at a place round the corner when he's had a word with them.'

'What does he think our chances are?' asked Laura as she took a seat beside Ian at the bar. Kim sat on the other side.

'I couldn't tell, and he wouldn't say outright,' Ian told them. 'He's not a man I'd like to play poker with!' he grinned, trying to look relaxed. 'Whatever can be done will be done. He's as good as Maxwell claimed, so we mustn't worry.'

He ordered a round of drinks and, while they waited to see what would happen next, Kim had a good look round, trying to take her mind off the outcome. She felt she would like to bring her sketch-pad in here with her some time. The building was old, maybe seventeenth-century, and in its day had been one of London's famous meeting-houses. A yellowing scroll in a case above the bar listed the historical figures known to have met here. Now the tiny timbered bar was full of goggling tourists. But at least the men from Jackpot weren't here.

She let Ian and Laura talk between themselves while she soaked in the atmosphere. Another glance round took in the oak-timbered roof beams, dark, well-worn wooden settles and sawdust floor. She was just wondering if it was real or only fake when a dark shape appeared on the other side of the glazed door to the street. She knew who it was even before he opened it. He shouldered his way through the crowd, his expression vexed, but he brightened as soon as his eyes lighted on Kim's upturned face. 'I'm afraid they're digging in their heels,' he announced as he came up beside her. 'Can't see why they're being so obstinate. They haven't a chance and they must have been told that—but there you are. They want a fight, so a fight is what they'll get!' After his initial annoyance, he seemed to relish the thought.

Ian looked glum. 'Why are they going on? They know they're in the wrong. There can't be any doubt.'

'Maybe I was too gentle with them this morning. Don't worry, there'll be no more pussyfooting around. They're simply mounting up costs for themselves. Some people are like that. They shut their eyes to the consequences and refuse to give in.'

His eyes, Kim registered, were blue, Irish blue, light and very bright. She still didn't know his name. She suddenly realised he was speaking to her. Hurriedly bending her head to catch what he said, she leaned forward just as he moved closer and they were brought into sudden fleeting contact, his cheek brushing her forehead, one hand skimming her shoulder. She felt he wanted to touch her more, his hands hovering around her, the red heat of attraction rocketing between them, but, evidently thinking better of it, he touched her glass with the tip of one finger.

'You're eating as well?'

'I don't know. What does Ian say?' Flustered, she turned, stepping back clumsily into the person behind, confused by the rush of feeling aroused by that fleeting physical contact, and trapped by the press of people crowding round them, cutting off any chance of drawing out of range.

'I have a table upstairs. We'll go up now,' he told her decisively. He explained to Ian and everyone trooped up after him. The decision, Kim noted, had obviously been made for them whether they liked it or not. She wondered what would happen if she objected and said she wanted a bag of crisps in the bar instead. Ian and Laura didn't seem to mind being organised. She tried to enter last to avoid getting too close to him, but the table for four was so small it made no difference. She felt her foot kick accidentally against his as she sat down, sending a shock-wave right through her body.

The secluded table they were at was evidently his regular one, and a waitress came up as soon as they walked in, obviously pleased to see a regular customer.

When she left Kim felt their host's eyes on her and she was vibrantly conscious of his hand lying only inches away from hers across the cloth. Striving to inject a note of normality into their encounter, she turned to Ian, saying, 'Don't you think it's about time you made a few introductions?'

Ian hit the side of his head with the flat of his hand. 'Sorry, folks. My mind's so full of Jackpot, everything else has gone to the wall.'

A hand reached for hers. 'Arlington—Con Arlington.'

'Con,' repeated Laura beside Kim before she herself could say anything. 'That won't be easy to forget.'

Kim gave a shudder, not only at the unexpected physical contact of the hand that held hers, but at the half-familiar name he announced. Long ago the name of the prosecuting lawyers had included an Arlington-Forbes, and even after all this time the name seemed to hold the ring of doom for her.

'Kim Wetherby, my partner,' Ian was saying, while Con Arlington went on holding her hand.

She felt his grip tighten. 'Partner? I'm so sorry— I didn't realise.' His expression had changed slightly. The eyes, endlessly deep, seemed to stare straight into her soul. Still he held her hand. She felt the tension mount inside her, and it took all her reserves to disengage her fingers from that powerful grasp. His touch made her whole body flame.

She smiled and gave a little toss of her dark mane to ease him back into perspective. 'Arlington,' she repeated, and then, as if to explain away her obvious confusion, she went on, 'I once had a bitter experience with a law firm named Arlington. But that was Arlington-Forbes.' She gave a quick grin and pretended to shiver. The blue eyes were gazing distantly into hers as if reading something very small written in her face.

When he spoke his voice seemed to come from miles away. 'Actually I am Arlington-Forbes. I dropped the Forbes for brevity.' His expression was inscrutable. 'What was the case you were involved in?'

'It was between my parents,' Kim explained as briefly as possible. 'They battled for custody for years. And then there was a dispute over some property.'

'Wetherby versus Flaxton?' he asked with a curious lift of his dark brows.

'You've heard of it?' she asked, surprised.

'Naturally. It did drag on, that one, didn't it? Finally finishing up in the High Court, so I believe.'

Kim nodded.

'It was one of those bitter family feuds that drag on for years,' he remarked, narrowing his eyes. Then he turned those oceans of warm blue on her. 'So you're the daughter?'

She nodded again, too stunned to speak.

He gave a sad, bitter smile. 'There's always an innocent party.'

'How do you know so much about the case?' she asked cautiously.

He hesitated before speaking. When he did so his eyes were veiled. 'I took it on from one of my uncles. I was in chambers with him after my pupilage, and that one was one of my first briefs.'

Kim gave a small gasp and rose to her feet. 'It can't be! You? Are you saying it was you five years ago...you're the Arlington-Forbes who...' Then she gripped the side of the table as she felt the room recede. Everything seemed to tilt and with an enormous effort she took a deep breath and drew herself up.

'I can't stay—I'm sorry.' She began to push past Laura whose chair was wedging hers in the corner. 'I must get out!'

Scarcely knowing how her legs were carrying her, she stumbled round the edge of the table and made for the door. Somewhere behind her she heard a voice tell her to come back, but with a gasp of emotion she fled towards the exit.

CHAPTER TWO

HE CAUGHT up with her when she was half-way down the stairs. She felt a hand snatch out to grasp her shoulder and she was pulled bodily to a halt. He descended until they were standing on the same tread, he hulking over her, not releasing his grasp.

'It was five years ago,' he told her, unable to keep the impatience out of his voice.

'Yes! You know that. You remember it, of course. It would be engraved on your heart if you had one!'

'I have a very good memory.'

'Do you sleep at night?'

'So, you lost a house.' He shrugged. 'What was it called, East Leigh?'

'Don't! It wasn't the house——' Her throat closed in a sudden spasm of emotion, cutting off her words, and hot tears brimmed in her eyes. Someone pushed past on their way up to the restaurant, giving them both a strange look as they did so.

'We can't stand here.' Without asking her Con Arlington pulled her down to the bottom of the stairs, pushing her ahead into the courtyard outside. There was an alley leading between the huddle of buildings and he bundled her round the corner out of sight of the passers-by before she could resist.

21

Chaotic feelings tumbled her thoughts all over as his very proximity sent her pressing back against the brick wall to escape the slightest physical contact with him, an instinctive sense of danger warning her to keep as far away from him as she could.

He placed a hand flat on the wall beside her head to prevent any escape, not touching her, but effectively trapping her so that he could look down into her face. She could feel the cuff of his pinstripe jacket brushing her hair.

'Kim Wetherby.' The blue eyes scudded over her face. 'You must be twenty-two now. I thought you were about seventeen when I saw you in the bar last night. Not that I knew who you were. Underage drinking, I thought. I couldn't take my eyes off you—not because you looked so young, but because you reminded me of someone. Now I know who it was—it was that young beauty in the Press-cuttings file when I was reading up about the case. I thought then I...' He left the sentence unfinished. 'Your cheeks are flushed, Kim. Is it anger?'

She nodded.

'Why?' he looked puzzled. 'What is there to be angry about after all this time?' The blue eyes raked her face for an answer and when she didn't reply he brought up his other hand and caught one of the tears she was unable to blink back, tracing its path with one finger down her cheek, and when it was dry, letting his finger remain where it was, feathering her skin, taunting her senses with the thought of what he would do next.

'Anger,' he considered, 'yes, and something else?' He traced a slow path to her lips, outlining the full curve of them with the tip of one finger, while she held herself rigidly controlled, fighting the seductive trail of his touch.

His voice dropped to a whisper. 'Is it something to do with me? Things seemed fine until you discovered who I was.' He tracked the path of her tear again, thoughtfully, assessingly, then shook his head, dismissing the thought. 'No, that couldn't be possible. You wouldn't harbour feelings like this after five years. And the court's decision can't have caused much hardship. You can't feel like this over a mere house, however beautiful. There must be something else.'

When she didn't answer immediately he gave an impatient shrug. 'I was only doing my job, you know!'

'Your *job*?' Kim ground out, managing to find her voice at last. 'Don't talk to me in that smug way about doing your job. You ruined my mother! You destroyed her as surely as if you'd stuck a knife into her heart! Don't talk to me about your job, Mr Arlington-Forbes.'

'The name's Conan, Con to my friends.'

'Con!' she spat. 'How appropriate! If there were a hell you would burn in it!'

She flicked her head sideways, ducking under the arm barring her escape, but he was quick enough to stop her, dragging her back, accidentally slamming her body against the wall as she lost her balance. Both his arms came round her and for a split second she felt the solid length of him pressing against her. Unbidden desire screamed through her soul, his blue eyes brilliant with an answering light, but he released her, abruptly taking a step back and gesturing with one hand towards the end of the alley as if to permit her to leave.

He was breathing heavily. 'I'm sorry—that's not the usual way I handle my clients.' He ran a hand through his thick black hair and she caught a wild look in his eyes, quickly hidden by a glint of ironic humour.

'You astonish me!' she replied in a voice like black ice. 'I wouldn't put anything past a ruthless bastard like you.'

His response was swift. 'You'll be pleased I'm ruthless this afternoon when I stand up in court and win your case for you!'

'I'll never be pleased by anything *you* can do!' she snarled.

'Is that so?' he murmured, dropping his voice to an intimate whisper. 'I wouldn't be too sure about that. All I need is time—and then I'm sure I could please you very much indeed.' His blue gaze washed over her like a caress.

For a moment Kim was bereft of words. Just looking at him she was sure he was right . . . but if there was anyone less likely to be welcomed in the role of lover it was this destroying, arrogant specimen standing in front of her.

With an effort she managed to grind out her reasons. 'I've hated the name Arlington-Forbes for five whole years,' she told him, surprised that, now she had the chance to escape, something held her here. She swayed slightly at the deliberate look of amusement that swept his face, as if he had trouble believing such a claim. His self-confidence was monumental! 'What you did to us, I can never forgive. So don't waste time giving me the works now—there's nothing to be gained.' She took a breath, wanting to cut the encounter short and to get as far away as she could, but now she had the chance something still kept her there.

'Permit me to be the judge of my losses and gains,' he said huskily, moving a pace closer.

'I'm surprised you admit to any losses. I wouldn't have thought that was your style.'

'I try to avoid them wherever possible.' His eyes didn't leave her face, but as if recalling himself to the present he thrust a hand into the pocket of his black pinstripe waistcoat and took out a watch. Only then did he tear his glance away. 'If you want something to eat before the afternoon session,' he slipped the watch back into his pocket and she was drowning in blue again, 'I suggest you come back to the restaurant straight away. What's past is past. I'm sorry if I've caused you any distress.'

'Distress?' Her lip curled and she drew herself up. 'One surprise after another,' she told him in her most cutting tones. 'I accept your apology for being an out-and-out bastard, Mr Arlington-

Forbes, but understand one thing, I would rather
eat poison than sit down at the same table with a
man like you!' And with a swish of her dark hair
she turned her back and marched straight out into
the main street.

He didn't try to stop her. She didn't even know
if he came out after her or not. Without a backward
glance she made her way on to the street and dived
into the first café she saw.

When she finally sat down, after fuming in a self-
service queue for five minutes, she noticed with de-
tachment that her hands were still shaking. Of
course it's anger, she told herself. Anger, anger, and
nothing but anger. Con Arlington is everything I
always knew he was—smug, opinionated, ruthless,
ambitious. A man with a block of ice where a heart
should be. Thank goodness the case will soon be
over, then I shall teach myself to forget I ever set
eyes on such a specimen.

If she saw much more of him she wouldn't trust
herself not to do something drastic. Then she would
really need a lawyer.

When Kim slipped back into her seat beside
Laura in the public gallery the court was already
in session. She deliberately delayed her return in
order to avoid bumping into Con Arlington, as he
seemed to be called now, feeling unable to trust
herself not to lose control should she see him
sweeping down the corridors towards her. The usher
let her in just as the defence lawyer sat down. 'Our
man', she thought ironically as he rose to his feet

and his gaze made a self-confident sweep of the court.

It was agonising to be forced to watch him in action now, making magnificent mincemeat of the opposition, tearing their defence to shreds, and as a sideline, having the court in roars of laughter with his perfectly timed remarks at the witnesses' expense, demonstrating to even the most sceptical what a tissue of lies the defence had been.

No wonder Mother lost her case so resoundingly, Kim thought as she watched and listened. Con Arlington was supremely sure of himself, with a brain like quicksilver to back him up. Even if he was entirely in the wrong, as he had been five years ago, he was the sort who could twist anything to mean exactly what he wanted. Her mother's words, spoken all those years ago, came back.

She had been in court for weeks and looked bone-weary as she came back to the rented cottage in Cornwall that weekend. 'They sent in a young Daniel against my old lion of a barrister, my dear. No one expected a battle—it seemed such a straightforward issue. My man has years of experience, it should have been a walkover. After all, we are in the right. But I suppose that was the trouble—he was just too sure of himself.' She had settled wearily into her favourite chair beside the open window. The sea moaned restlessly beneath the cliff. 'The younger man, give him credit, was superb. He'd really boned up on all the ins and outs of the case, then he produced some dusty old precedent clinching the verdict...in favour of your father. That's that, my dear.' She closed her eyes.

'Mum, I don't believe it! They can't take our home away from us!' Kim, at seventeen, had been immeasurably shocked. She remembered clinging to her mother, crying over and over, 'I won't let them! They can't! I just won't let them!'

'They can and they have,' her mother replied, stroking her hair. 'I'll never forget the face of the judge when he came to sum up. It held sheer admiration. It'll be the making of that young man.' She paused. 'And the unmaking of us, my darling. Your father has got his hands on East Leigh at last.'

'But it's sheer spite. He doesn't want it—he'll never live there.'

'He wants it because you chose me,' her mother said sadly. 'And the law says he has a legal right to live in the house that's been in my family for four generations. From today I become a trespasser in the house that was once my home, a trespasser in my own gardens.' Then, remembered Kim with a shudder, she added something else. 'After this, after the endless years of lawsuits and counterlawsuits, losing East Leigh is the last straw for me.'

Those last were the words that caused Kim most pain now. In retrospect she should have seen what they meant. But at seventeen she was too young to understand. It had been enough that after years of being separated by the courts she and her mother were together again at long last. They had that at least.

Kim came back to the present with a jolt. Laura was shaking her by the arm. 'Dead boring when *he* stops talking, isn't it?' she whispered in Kim's ear. The defence lawyer was droning on again, but it was obvious from his demeanour that he was scraping the bottom of the barrel. There was really nothing more to be said.

A glance towards the back rows of the wooden seats showed the two men from Jackpot sitting staring straight ahead with tight-lipped expressions, and Laura pretended to shudder. 'Thank goodness this isn't Sicily,' she joked, then, 'Kim, you're looking as grim as they are! Is it to do with what happened at lunchtime? Con said you were feeling under the weather. We thought you must have decided to skip lunch. Can——'

'Silence in the gallery!' a voice interrupted from behind them.

'Tell me later,' hissed Laura, turning round to give a brilliant smile at the policeman who had ticked her off.

They came out of the court-room some time later with differing expressions on their faces. The judge had decided to adjourn until the next morning when he would give his summing up and judgement. Laura was unperturbed, bubbling over as usual, confident that everything would eventually swing their way. Ian, naturally enough, was showing signs of strain. 'How are we supposed to sleep tonight, with this hanging over our heads?' Kim, though she shared these views, was rather more dismayed than she had expected.

Then she made a decision. 'I'll go back home tonight. We can't leave the others to run the studio for another day without one of us around. What if something important crops up?'

'I thought you wanted to have a couple of days in London with your friend Lizzie,' said Ian. 'Heaven knows, you deserve a break, Kim.'

'I'm not just being noble, Ian. I simply can't face that man again.'

'Which man?' broke in Laura, who had only been half listening.

'Arlington-Forbes.' It was all she could do to utter his name.

'I don't care what he did in the past, Kim, there's no getting away from the fact that he's a dish,' asserted Laura with complete lack of tact.

'I'd call him rather florid, actually,' retorted Kim. 'Too much good living. He'll be overweight by the time he's forty.'

'That's not what you were saying this morning!'

'That was before I knew what a—who he was.' She averted her head, fists bunched.

'Agree on floridly handsome, then? I'll give you that much.'

'Shut up, Laura!' broke in Ian edgily. 'Can't you be quiet? You're so stupid sometimes!'

Laura gasped. Ian had never spoken to her like that before.

He went on, 'Can't you see Kim's not in the mood to talk about him right now? Use your imagination, can't you?' His face registered the concern he felt as he came over to Kim and put an arm round her. 'Don't be upset, love. It's not worth it now. It's all over.'

She felt a deep pain over something she had imagined was long since buried and to her shame tears began to trickle silently down her cheeks. She was all emotion today, it seemed. Bending her head, she snuffled apologetically into Ian's shoulder, trying to hide her face from the passers-by.

Ian led her outside. 'There, there, lamb, it's all right.' He gave her a warm hug and she felt relieved that at least somebody knew the full story and could guess at the turmoil she was in. His hand stroked the top of her head, pressing it briefly against his shoulder.

Then a voice like cut-glass pierced Ian's gentle reassurances.

'Goodbye, Robertson—everyone. See you in the morning.'

Kim recognised the voice. How could she not? She looked over her shoulder in time to see Con Arlington-Forbes striding down the steps of the court building, his black silk fluttering with the speed of his departure as he made his way across the square towards his chambers.

He turned to look back at the trio on the steps before he reached the corner, and for a man who had yet another success within his grasp he was

looking surprisingly angry, the dark face made
darker by the glowering expression on it. He seemed
to have second thoughts about leaving so abruptly,
though, for he suddenly spun and began to walk
purposefully back towards them, coming to a halt
when he reached the bottom of the steps again. He
looked up.

'Don't worry about all this. It's open and shut.
The judge simply wants to cogitate a while on how
much it's going to cost them.' He gave a half-
hearted smile, his eyes flicking from one to the
other.

Kim's face was dry now, but she knew she must
look washed out. Con's eyes were now focused on
her, boring into her face and looking bluer than she
would have thought possible. It was like an af-
front, the way he was appraising her as if he were
recording every flickering change of expression in
that computerised brain of his. He could tell she
had been crying, judging by the look of alarm that
came on to his face. He would be a man who hated
tears, weakness.

Kim drew herself up, tucking one arm into Ian's.
'Let's go—I'm tired of hanging round here.' Head
erect, she marched down the steps beside Ian,
sweeping past Con without a glance. No, she vowed,
she would not return in the morning. The sooner
she could get out of London, the better.

Ian and Laura stayed on at the hotel they had
booked into the previous night and Kim went back

to Lizzie's flat in South Kensington to tell her of her change of plan.

'We're told we'll win, but whether costs will have to be shared is something we shall only learn tomorrow. It's not worth my while losing a day in the studio. Ian and Laura will let me know what happens soon enough.' She kept quiet about Con Arlington—she didn't feel comfortable using his name, even. It made her want to choke with dislike. Fortunately Lizzie didn't suffer from curiosity, and if she noticed Kim's rather subdued manner she said nothing. She did try to persuade her to stay the night, though, travelling back first thing in the morning, but the thought of staying in the same city with him was anathema. She knew it was stupid, but she couldn't help it.

It was a relief to go to work next morning and carry on as if everything were normal. Outwardly things *were* normal—it was only in her heart that a seismic reaction had set in.

When Ian rang at half past eleven he was jubilant. 'He's done it! We don't pay a penny. They were held entirely responsible! 'Struth, Kim, it isn't half a relief. I wasn't relishing the thought of coughing up any of our hard-earned profits at this stage!'

'Now we can get on with some work, I suppose,' commented Kim, unable to share fully in Ian's triumph. She tried again, searching her mind for something positive to say. She felt like a used dish-cloth, a feeling out of all proportion to what had happened. 'A nice commission came in while we were away, Ian—only a little one, but it's for a shoe factory at Lower Marsh. They want a leaflet. I thought I might go out there this afternoon. May as well get started straight away and——'

'No,' he broke in, 'don't leave the studio——' He hesitated, sounding guarded as he added, 'Something interesting has come up. I'd like you around so that I can make a few phone calls after I've spoken to you.'

'What? This sounds very mysterious.'

'Yes, let's leave it there. How's everything else progressing?' Ian changed the subject. 'Any problems?'

'No. Ron seems to have coped quite well. Sue came in for an hour or so. She's finished those drawings for the furniture exhibition.'

'Good girl. Tell her so from me!' He rang off after that and Kim returned to her drawing-board.

She had joined Ian two years ago, six months after he had set up the one-man band that in those days was all Image Design was. Together they produced publicity material for small local firms, most of it routine stuff, but some of it requiring Kim's special drawing skills and, more recently, photographs.

Ian himself was a talented draughtsman, but rather than work for someone else he had been determined to set up on his own. It was a series of his own technical drawings for an engineering firm that had been stolen, used and actually put together in a pamphlet by the only other publicity firm in the area of any note. He suspected it had happened before, but it had been difficult to prove. With the two rivals going after the same account it was easy to see how Bill and Dick Renfrew of Jackpot had got hold of the newer company's designs—they could have been left lying about on someone's desk when they visited the engineering firm, and the temptation to pick them up and pass them off as their own must have been too great. The suspicion had soured things between the two rivals, turning what had seemed friendly competition into something much more bitter.

It was only through a friend, working in the drawing office of the firm concerned, and recognising Ian's work, that the truth had come out. It explained, too, why they had failed to land that particular commission when Ian had been sure they would get it. When the court's verdict became public there were going to be red faces at the engineering company, as it was the carelessness of one of their own employees that had contributed to the situation, no doubt.

Curious to know why Ian had been so mysterious over the phone, Kim speculated idly on what it could be about. Obviously it was work of some sort. But how on earth had he managed to scrape anything up in the few hours since she had last seen him? Of course, he was a go-getter, despite his unassuming manner. It was only Laura who seemed to run rings round him. Smiling to herself, she finished a mock-up for the brochure of a new health club. It would need photographs, she considered, but Ian had been adamant that she stay in the studio this afternoon.

Ron came through about three. 'They've arrived. And they've got someone with them.' He hefted the postbag on to the counter and began to frank the letters inside. A part-timer came in to help Laura with the secretarial work when things got busy. They were still at the stage of make or break, teetering on the edge of acquiring a really big commission that would give them credibility and a greater measure of financial security.

Kim scarcely looked up. They had made good time on the way back—no doubt Laura had been driving. But they would hardly have had time to go and pick up Ian's father. Now retired, he took a lively interest in the day-to-day running of the business, and, Kim knew, had sunk quite a lot of his retirement money into it too. He would be the first person to whom Ian would want to announce the verdict.

'You know what Ian's dad looks like, don't you, Ron?' she asked, barely looking up, absorbed in her work.

'Sure, why?'

Her head jerked up. 'You mean there's somebody else with them?'

Before she could move the door flew open and Ian sauntered into the room, followed at once by

Laura. There was a pause, then a sickeningly familiar shape hove into view.

Kim half rose, pencil falling from her grasp. The noise as it hit the floor, bounced, then rolled under a chair seemed deafening in the silence that heralded the entrance of the third person. Kim gritted her teeth and felt her hackles rise. What was Con Arlington-Forbes doing in her domain?

She came swiftly round the side of her desk, her senses on red alert at the very sight of him.

'What's he doing here?' she croaked, with no effort to be polite.

Ian looked as pleased as Punch. 'I told you over the phone, love. We've got a commission.'

CHAPTER THREE

'I WANTED you here, Kim, because I was going to put something to you and then ring Con to let him know what you thought,' Ian told her, 'but when I said you might be difficult to persuade he said he'd come over himself.'

'Very kind,' Kim murmured distantly. It was laughable! The man was so puffed up with his own conceit, he actually believed he could talk her into fitting in with his plans. She gave a thin smile and looking directly at him said, '*He* couldn't talk me into anything, I'm afraid. What a pity he's had a wasted journey.' She turned back to her desk, effectively dismissing the three of them, and reaching out for her pencil, remembering too late that it had fallen to the floor when Con Arlington-Forbes came in. Now he bent to retrieve it, handing it back without a word, his face wiped of all expression.

The silence seemed to go on and on. Ian and Laura were staring at her in amazement, and for their benefit rather than anyone else's she heard herself saying, 'Pity you've come all this way for nothing, Mr Arlington-Forbes. But no doubt someone will show you round before you go back, to make the journey worth your while.'

Her head was bent, but she felt him move forward until he was standing just in front of her. 'I'm not going back. Not until you've listened to what I have to say. Ian thinks my proposal's a good one.'

'Good? I leaped at it. No playing Mr Cool with an offer like this!' Ian stepped forward, putting both hands on the edge of her drawing-board.

Kim lifted her head, eyeing both men suspiciously, then turned to Laura. 'Maybe you'd be kind enough to translate for Mr Arlington-Forbes? Would you tell him I'm not interested in anything in any way connected with him. He's fully aware of my reasons. I stand by those. The matter's closed.'

'Oh, *do* listen!' exclaimed Laura at once. 'You must at least listen, Kim. It's a golden opportunity for us all.'

Kim gaped at her. What had happened to solidarity? She felt like quipping about knives in the back, but instead she said, 'Opportunity? For what? A nice fat fee?' She felt a weak laugh escape her. 'I'll do more or less anything for Image Design, as you both know, but everyone has their limit. This is mine.'

She saw Ian's fist clench on top of the desk, but he didn't say anything. Instead Con Arlington-Forbes—the name wounded like a knife—nodded to him and said quickly, 'Leave this to me.'

Before Kim could bat an eyelid both Ian and Laura, and, after a short, bewildered pause, Ron, filed out of the studio. She could hear them go into the rest-room next door and the sound of cups and saucers was only cut off when her hated antagonist slammed the door shut between them.

'I don't know what you want, but count me out!' she flared as soon as he turned to face her.

Instead of lashing back he gave a rueful smile and went over to one of the windows, where he stood looking out for a moment or two while Kim waited for him to go on, and when he turned back he was still smiling. But she was ready for him. She clenched her fists and moved forward. 'I don't know what private arrangement you've made with Ian, or indeed what dubious job you want him to do,' she started fiercely, 'but as his partner I can understand he would want it cleared with me first— Ian's like that,' she gave a deprecating smile, 'considerate, fair, reasonable. Something you wouldn't understand. And he knows how I feel about getting involved with you, so I can see you've been very clever to get him on your side. Normally,' she continued swiftly as he seemed about to interrupt, 'I'd be willing to go along with him—but this time, no way.'

She paused, annoyed to find he wasn't bothering to defend himself. Obviously he knew it was useless. 'I suppose you have to save face by appearing to be trying to talk me into agreeing.' She leaned comfortably against her drawing-board. 'I don't mind sitting it out for a few minutes so that you can save face. Be my guest, Mr Arlington-Forbes.'

'Quite a comic, aren't you?' He lifted his sleek dark head. Kim was disconcerted to find that instead of the anger of defeat suffusing his face he was actually smiling again as if everything were a huge joke. He copied her actions now, lounging against the windowsill, very much at ease. 'The name,' he went on, 'is Con Arlington. But I suppose if you insist on this rather quaint formality Mr Arlington will do.'

'What I call you is neither here nor there, as you'll be leaving soon and I hope we never need meet again.'

'Oh, I need to meet you again, Kim Wetherby. Again and again and again.' His voice sank to a seductive bass, making her dauntingly aware of how attractive she had found him on first meeting. But she had no intention of weakly giving in to his practised charm now she knew who and what he was.

She gave a short laugh. 'Very good, Mr Arlington. I can almost see what it is that makes you such a successful advocate. You can turn on whatever technique will give you the upper hand. The only trouble is that in this case the defendant will fail to succumb.'

'Defendant? What are you defending, Kim?'

'I didn't mean——!' She blushed violently with an intuition that he could see straight into her heart—and she would die rather than have its contents revealed to him!

'Let me tell you what I think you're defending,' he continued. 'I think you're defending a blind prejudice against me because I happened to be instrumental to your mother's come-uppance.'

Kim stared at him in astonishment. 'How dare you say such a thing?' Her mouth worked. 'How *dare* you!' A tornado of emotion raged through her and she thrust herself round the side of the drawing-board, skidding to a halt only when it dawned on her how physically formidable he was and how unworried by her outburst. He no doubt faced more violent outbursts every day of his life in court. Her hands fell uselessly to her sides. Striving to control herself, she managed to choke back her anger and in tones like broken glass asked, 'What leads you to imagine she needed a come-uppance?' Then, not interested in his reply because it would be so outrageously wrong, she went on, 'After all those years trying to get custody of me after the courts reversed their original decision, after all those years fighting for what little she ever had, come-uppance is the very last thing justice should have dealt out. You, of course, despite your pretensions, have no interest in justice. The only thing concerning you is how to bulldoze your way to whatever result you decide you want.' Her piquant face with its frame of wild curls expressed every bit of the scorn she felt.

Once again she saw his face blank out any expression and the cool blue eyes raked her as objectively as a buyer in a market. She shivered with rage at the silent insult.

Before she could say anything he said, 'Are you trying to tell me she wasn't the greedy, empty-headed, over-privileged woman I was told she was? On the point of marrying a millionaire when you were ten—do correct me if my memory is at fault—she was quite happy to hand you back to your father. When that relationship failed also it suited her to entice you back to live with her—in the hope that it would ensure her possession of East Leigh. I'm sorry to be so brutal, but it was—do correct me——' he invited again, 'your grandfather's bequest to you, to be held in trust until your twenty-first birthday.'

'But the court overrode Grandpa's wishes, giving the house to my father instead.'

'To be held by him, for you, until——'

'To be sold by him, for himself, for revenge!' Kim burst in.

'Not if you were living there.'

'Living there? Are you mad? Do you think I could have lived in that house with that man and his paramour? Don't you understand anything? No,' she broke in before he could answer, 'you wouldn't understand how the head can be ruled by the heart. And I suppose you think that's stupid—that I deserved to lose East Leigh for being so emotional. Well, I'm not sorry about that. I do have feelings. And I'd rather lose everything and be true to my feelings than be a cold, heartless monster like you!' Then before he could interrupt she went on, 'And you're so wrong about all this. That's not the way it was. I expect you had to listen to him, and he's as plausible a monster as you are yourself, but in the cause of justice I would have thought you would have had a passing interest in the other side of the story.'

'I was briefed on the case from its inception.'

'Yes! By my father!'

'Don't forget my uncle handled most of your father's affairs when you were a child.'

'But you still only got one side of it!'

'I'm sure it was the truth.'

'Sure? How can you be sure?' Kim turned away with an expression of disgust. 'I've been right to hate you all these years. What else would you be like? It'd be stupid to expect anything else from a man like you, who sells himself daily to anybody who's prepared to pay his price! If you were a woman there'd only be one word for you!'

Suddenly he was hulking over her, and a shiver of fright ran up her spine. He was so close, a scent of Russian leather swamping her senses, and she felt her limbs become as soft as cotton wool until she managed to drag herself together, stepping back with a weak, 'Don't,' putting out her hands to defend herself as if she expected a physical assault.

He moved closer, following her, pace for pace. 'You have a marvellous opinion of me, Kim Wetherby. First you insult my vocation and then you cower back as if you expect me to give you the hiding you deserve.' His blue eyes licked over her face with a message his words didn't contain. Affronted and caressed at the same moment, she began to tremble in confusion. A hand put up to smooth back a loose tress fell back to grasp the edge of the desk for support.

'Don't come near me,' she ground out, already feeling her own body's betrayal as it softened with yearning towards his. 'You and your uncle treated Mother diabolically. But what did you ever care? As long as you got your fee. You were paid to do and say whatever Father requested. You were nothing but his paid lackey!'

More than anything else she had said so far, this seemed to affect Con Arlington the most. He shuddered to a stop only a few inches from her, his face visibly whitening, whether with rage or with shock at her candour she couldn't tell, but she could at least see the muscles of his body in the expensive dark suit tauten with suppressed energy of some kind.

When he spoke his lips scarcely moved. 'Do you imagine you're the only one with a limit you won't go past?' He drew his lips back in a harsh laugh. 'Don't presume so much, my dear.' He flicked a tendril of hair from out of her eyes, murmuring in a voice made breathy with a sudden thrill, 'I wonder if you're as incorruptible as you pretend.'

He stopped talking and let his cool blue eyes explore her upturned face, her green ones glittering in response at the prospect of combat, cheeks flushing at such objective scrutiny. Then his glance inched down a little, noting with sardonic amusement the rise and fall of her breasts beneath the thin cotton blouse as she struggled for control, her breath rasping audibly in and out as he moved closer still.

'I would say, Miss Wetherby, if asked,' he murmured, lowering his head so that his words fell like a whisper in her ear, 'that you're very close to the point where you could be persuaded to go well beyond the limits you set yourself. For no price at all,' he added insultingly. He lifted his head a little to gauge her response. 'Would you not agree?'

The crack of her palm across his left cheek gave a report like a pistol-shot. The effect was nearly as dramatic. He gave a short exclamation, stepped back, one hand to his cheek, and then, without seeming to move at all, reached out, grasping her roughly by a handful of hair at the back of the neck and bringing his body crushing against hers so that she couldn't repeat her attack. As he pressed her helplessly against the edge of the drawing-board his eyes glittered like shards of ice, the red imprint of her hand deepening down the side of his face.

For a moment she thought he was going to give her the same treatment, and her sharp, frightened intake of breath was the prelude to expected punishment, but to her intense surprise the cold objectivity of his expression, the anger that had just then distorted his face, gave way to a sudden softening, a look of puzzlement, an expression almost of hurt, worse than any chastisement. It was quickly concealed, but he said softly, 'I don't want this, Kim. We don't have to fight. And I don't want to have to defend myself against physical assault every time I come close to you.' His voice vibrated with emotion. 'But if you're going to attack me at every turn I shall have to find a way of stopping you.' His grip tightened in warning and she was in no doubt that he would carry out whatever threat seemed appropriate.

'Don't come close then, bully!' She tried to twist from side to side, but he held her in a grasp that hurt when she moved.

'Even you know I'm no bully.' He shifted his weight, effectively pinning her in his arms, but with no grounds to claim he was hurting her now. His hand buried itself in the tangle of dark hair, caressing her with a slow, sensual touch at the same time as it tilted her face at just the angle he wanted. She yearned and feared at the same moment for the kiss she knew was going to come. Her body spoke its own desire as it softened against his. Its meaning did not escape him.

For a long moment, a moment out of time, their souls spoke silently to each other, all differences forgotten, echoes of buried desire drowning her protests as his lips came down with slow deliberation, coaxing into submission any remnant of opposition, beguiling her senses with promises of heaven. His kiss deepened, his tongue probing heatedly into the unexplored cavern, his fingers releasing the tension of resistance so that she was melting, swooning with the unexpected madness of need. It was as if she had reached safe haven to experience such intimacy.

A sound outside the door alerted them to the presence of a world beyond this newly summoned one of their own.

'My lovely Kim, this is how it's got to be. I knew it would be heaven to touch your lips. Kiss me again——'

'Someone's coming in. I—Con...' She avoided his questing lips with a wild look. 'I don't want you to——'

Then the door did open and Ian stepped through. As his glance fell on the two of them, Con was already moving back to the other side of the desk. Kim turned her head, striving to appear unruffled, her mind a whirlwind of confusion.

'Any agreement?' asked Ian innocently, looking from one to the other. Seeing Kim's flushed face, he gave a grimace, and evidently thinking she was still violently opposed to the proposal, said, 'Maybe if you have time to think about it?'

Kim glanced quickly from one to the other, wishing Con would come to her aid. What would Ian say if he knew the nature of their 'discussion'? Surely he could see the reality written on her face?

Con raised his sleek head, his face as cool, as astonishingly in control as ever, no sign of its having dwelt in paradise for a few brief moments, and said, 'Of course she'll agree. But I haven't finished outlining it yet. What about coming out to the car, Kim? We'll drive somewhere. It's early, but I'm sure we can stop for afternoon tea and go over the details at our leisure.' His glance covered hers before turning to Ian.

Kim was doubly confused. Did he think he had the right to assume she would agree to something he hadn't even explained? And, what was worse, did he imagine she was so naïve, so bowled over by the fact that the great Con Arlington had actually kissed her, that she would say yes to whatever else he suggested? Was this what he thought she meant about limits? And did he imagine she had so easily and supinely reached hers?

'Wait a moment.' Easing herself away from the support of the drawing-board, she stepped forward, saying, 'I still don't know how I'm supposed to be involved in all this.'

Ian raised his eyebrows in surprise and Con cut in smoothly with, 'That's what we'll discuss over tea.'

But Ian looked puzzled. 'What have you been talking about, then? I thought——'

'We had to find some common ground first,' remarked Con casually. He gave a satisfied smile. 'I think I speak for both of us when I say we seem to have achieved our aim.'

'Wait a minute.' Kim felt her old anger return. 'It would be unfair to raise Ian's hopes. We obviously have much to discuss, Mr Arlington. But I can't see why you can't give me a general idea of what your plans entail. I mean, has your proposal got anything to do with me directly or——?'

Ian broke in. 'You'll be the one to go, of course. It's way beyond my capabilities. And Con knows this. It'll be your assignment, but you'll be working under the umbrella of Image Design, of course.'

'Go?' She looked from one to the other.

'To Montpellier, of course,' Ian said impatiently. 'Haven't you told her anything?' Puzzled, his grey eyes flickered from one to the other before he directed the question at Con.

'I hadn't got that far,' Con told him. 'I didn't want her to say no.'

'I'm sorry, I didn't mean to come blundering in. I must admit,' chuckled Ian, 'I fully expected to hear the sound of smashing furniture!' He gave Kim a friendly pat on the shoulder. 'I know you'll be able to reach some sort of agreement, love. Wait till you hear the rest of it.' Turning to Con, he smiled and nodded with satisfaction. 'You two go off, then. Stitch it up and Laura'll get on to the airline before she leaves at five.'

'Airline? What the hell is this?' Kim wasn't pretending anger now. First Con's smug assumption that she was going to do what he wanted anyway, and now this!

'We've been offered an assignment to do a job for Con in the South of France. You'll have to go over this weekend to have a recce. Report back here early next week. We'll cost it out and if Con here OKs it you'll return the following weekend and spend however long you think necessary. Does that sum it up, Con?'

'It does indeed.' Con's eyes flickered with amusement when he saw Kim's outraged expression. 'Come on, Miss Wetherby. We need to talk.'

'You're damned right we need to talk!' Kim exclaimed when they got outside into the car park. She scarcely registered the car Con was leading her towards until she saw him go to the driver's door and unlock it.

'Where do you think we're going? I'm not going anywhere with you, not until—well, not any time.'

'Look,' he seemed impatient now, 'you'd agree we need to talk this out?'

She compressed her lips. It was the understatement of the century, but she wasn't going to say anything to give the impression she was agreeing with him.

'And you would probably admit you'd rather do it in private—than with your partner, secretary and assorted employees assessing the state of play from the ringside seat of the studio window?'

'What?' She half turned, then wished she hadn't. Laura was sitting on the sill, a smile of encouragement on her face when she noted Kim's glance.

'And further, you would admit, no doubt, that it'll be a darn sight more comfortable sitting inside this thing than standing out here in this blasted wind?'

'You're not in court now, Mr Arlington.' She nearly allowed herself a flicker of a smile, but the memory of his smug expression in the studio when he told Ian they had reached common ground made her conceal it from him. What he said was all true, though. When he came round to open the passenger door for her, she sank down into the red leather seat at once.

It was a sleek car, expensive and lethal, like Con Arlington himself. Feeling threatened by the power it implied, Kim huddled against the door, putting as much space between the two of them as possible. He slid the car into gear, and with a feeling that her bridges were being burned behind her she allowed him to drive her away from the safety of the studio.

'You know this area better than me,' he remarked as he swung out into the main road. 'Which way?'

'You weren't serious about afternoon tea?'

'Never more so. Why, doesn't the idea appeal?'

'Turn left, then. There's a farmhouse just before the next village.'

'Wonderful countryside, this part of East Anglia,' Con remarked conversationally. 'I wonder why I slog it out in central London.'

'Because that's where the streets are paved with gold.'

'Are they?' He gave her a quick glance, taking in her still flushed oval face, the long-lashed green eyes, the tangle of dark hair.

She registered the look. 'I'm not going to agree to this, Con—Mr Arlington,' she corrected, angry with herself for allowing him to see how she was changing towards him. 'I'm sorry if it upsets your plans.'

'Sorry nothing. You'd be delighted if you could upset the apple-cart. You'd like nothing better!'

'As I haven't a clue what this apple-cart of yours consists of, I'll reserve judgement,' she replied tartly. She lapsed into silence, making it clear she wanted the conversation, if any, to stick to the point, but Con Arlington obviously had other ideas. He talked amiably on all kinds of topics and she got the impression of a man who enjoyed life to the full.

After only a few minutes a sign in a hedge proclaiming 'Farmhouse Teas' made him slow the car just as she drew his attention to it.

'Thought you'd lost the power of speech there,' he teased as the car bumped along the lane. 'I would imagine you'd be quite an entertaining conversationalist—when you're not sulking.'

'Is this going to be the tone of our little tea-party?' she asked, giving him a cold glance.

'Truce, then?' His blue eyes washed over her.

'Strictly business,' she corrected.

He smiled. 'Thus leaving room for war if necessary?'

'Look, Mr Arlington. As far as I'm aware, you've brought me out here to talk about some commission you're offering Image Design. My partner seems to think I'm the one to handle it. Let's take it from there, all right?'

'Yet you've left out one of the most important obstacles—your entrenched objections even to considering the proposal.'

'I'm going to listen. It's up to you to persuade me.' She stopped, jerking a hand up. 'I mean——'

'Yes?' he murmured, eyes full of meaning. Switching off the ignition as the car came to rest in the farmyard, he leaned forward to gaze with mocking concern into her eyes.

With a muffled cry of annoyance Kim turned away, running her hands along the side of the door to find the catch. Nothing seemed to work. She fumbled helplessly at what she thought was the right one until she heard a rustle of movement as Con leaned close, reaching across, murmuring, 'Here, let me.' But then it seemed to take an age before his fingers finally released it, and in the time it took she was conscious of his breath against the side of her cheek and the enveloping warmth of his body against hers. She was effectively trapped and he knew it.

Stiffening, she turned her head to give him a look designed to keep him at a distance. His face was only a few inches from her own. For what seemed like an age she held her breath, waiting for him to do something to release them both from their statue-like stillness, vividly aware of his nearness drawing her even closer. She could see the fine texture of his lightly tanned skin and the way it tightened across his cheekbones, and the way the lips, full and mobile, contrasted softly with the definition of black brows, dark-lashed eyes, and then that ocean of blue into which she felt she could plunge forever.

With a snap the door opened. Con moved back. A rush of cold air swept inside. Then, in breathless confusion, Kim slid out from the pressuring body next to hers and regained her freedom, walking rapidly away from the car, leaving him to lock up and follow her into the building.

'Pretty,' he observed when he reached her side. He stooped under the lintel, narrowly avoiding a crack on the head from the low beams, but gazing appreciatively round the stylish interior with its flower prints, burnished copper glow, red tiles, log fire. 'Like a picture book.' His eyes swept hers with double meaning. Kim coloured, turning away as if not understanding that he was handing out a compliment, and pretended to give the place, one she had visited dozens of times before, a thorough inspection.

There were half a dozen scrubbed tables in what had been the original farmhouse kitchen, vases of wild flowers on each, comfortable cushioned chairs in intimate groups. Con took charge, ushering her over to a table for two beside a leaded window overlooking the herb garden. 'A regular haunt of yours, is it?'

Kim shook her head. She knew the couple who owned it, but she wasn't going to tell him that. The less he knew about her the better. It would only lead to more involvement. Let him cling to his misguided ideas. She wasn't going to be the one to enlighten him.

A girl came through, and after they had ordered scones with home-made jam and cream and a pot of coffee Kim gave Con a level glance and asked, 'Over to you then, Mr Arlington. What is this wonderful commission I'm going to have to turn down?'

CHAPTER FOUR

'ONE of my uncles, from the Arlington side of the family,' he began, his blue eyes adding an unspoken comment, 'owns a small village near Montpellier called Abbaye-sur-Lac.'

Kim restrained a small gasp. A villa was one thing, but a village? 'So?' she demanded, looking away.

'So, he's keen on restoration, that sort of thing. The village itself is rather interesting. It was built for Louis the Fourteenth as a place where silk tapestries could be made—from spinning the silk to dyeing, weaving, and producing the final object. This one and the two or three others built at the same time were probably the first comprehensive factory sites in Europe. Weavers' cottages were built round a square, and there are, of course, dyeing sheds, drying facilities, plus all the usual buildings of any village of the time—bakers, blacksmiths and so on, together with the remains of some potentially magnificent formal gardens.'

'I still don't see what all this has to do with Image Design.'

'Listen then, and I'll tell you.'

Kim stiffened at his tone. He was treating her like a small child, drawing out his explanation in this deliberately provoking way, then chiding her when she got impatient.

'Uncle might be a bit of an eccentric—but he had the idea of restoring the place to its original condition. As you can imagine, it's been knocked about a bit in the intervening centuries and there's a lot to be done. His ultimate idea is to lease the cottages to artists and writers and to preserve the tapestry-making units as a fully functioning museum.'

'Complete with fully functioning workers?'

'Of course.'

'Well,' Kim broke in, 'it all sounds absolutely fascinating.' She had finished her coffee and declined a second cup. Her scone lay untouched upon her plate. She glanced at the grandfather clock in the corner. 'I'm ready to go back when you are.'

'Don't you want to know where you come in?' asked Con.

'I think its obvious, isn't it?'

'Well?'

'The answer's still no.'

'Then let me fill in the details. Image Design will be responsible for keeping a complete visual record in photographs and drawings of every stage of the restoration work. During this period a brochure will be put out describing its virtues and offering studio space to people who might be interested. It's going to be an ongoing job, because of course the work will take a couple of years to complete, and after that there'll be a turnover of short leases on the village property requiring a regular up-date of publicity material.'

'It seems too big for us,' protested Kim. 'We've never handled anything on this scale. I can't imagine why you should come to us.'

'I came to you because while I was going into the affairs of Image Design in order to put your case across in court I realised what a lot of talent and potential there was in the outfit.' Con was rather short and obviously quickly lost patience with anyone who objected to being steamrollered.

Kim eyed him suspiciously. 'You were impressed?' Her suspicion that it was a devious method of compromising her in some way rang in her voice. Flattery, he seemed to think, would get him anywhere, but she knew what had impressed *him*.

'I was impressed by Ian Robertson in particular,' he went on, confounding her expectations with a little smile. 'He's got his head screwed on. I would back his judgement. He's a shrewd feller and he's worked out one or two angles already.'

'I don't have to be told Ian knows what he's doing. I've worked with him for two years,' she bit back, piqued that she seemed merely incidental in the package. 'And as he's so shrewd, I'm sure he can pick out somebody else to cope with the technical side of the operation. There are plenty of people around who can wield a camera.'

'True. But he thinks very highly of your work, and actually I know Uncle is looking for someone

who's more than just a photographer. An artist is
what he wants. Someone who can turn out some
decent sketches and maybe a painting or two. Who
better than the daughter of Karla Wetherby?'

'I thought you told me she was just an empty-
headed, greedy, over-privileged woman?' Kim
sparked back. 'You can't have it all ways.'

'No one doubted she was a painter of note. But,
as so often with people of talent, she squandered
it in a crazy, self-indulgent life-style.'

'How do *you* know how she lived?' She half rose.
'I'm sick of being force-fed your stupid opinions.
You don't know a damned thing!'

'All right, we'll discuss that later,' Con told her
imperiously. 'What concerns us is your ability to
handle the commission. If you can't, we're going
to have to approach another company. Ian won't
be pleased at losing the fee. I've already talked
terms with him.'

'He can take on someone else to do what you
want,' she retorted.

'No way. They might turn out to be duds, and
I'm not going to pick up the tab for incompetence.'

'Are you trying to say the deal's off unless I per-
sonally say yes?'

He nodded, adding, 'I wasn't aware I was *trying*
to say anything. Let me put it even more clearly.
Unless you accept, now, I'm driving straight back
to town. You can explain to Robertson yourself that
you've lost him a fee for——' and then he named

a figure that made Kim blink despite her efforts to remain composed.

'It's a sort of blackmail, isn't it? I suppose I should expect that from someone like you. You spend your life defending the indefensible. It must be impossible to recognise criminal behaviour when you see it.'

His eyes turned to blue ice. 'Are you suggesting I'm breaking some law or other?'

'Heavens,' she gave a little laugh, acting for all she was worth, 'you're looking at me as if I'm slandering you! As if I'd dare!' She put a hand in mock helplessness to her lips. What game was he playing? His expression was spine-chilling. A look like that must strike terror into the hearts of his opponents. What was worse, he had won—she knew it. But he insisted on spelling it out, making her cast around in desperation to try to find a way out.

He said, 'Naturally I've got a good idea of your present turnover, and although you've done very well so far you need a big fat commission to enable you to change from being just another pint-sized outfit into the dynamically successful concern you could be. It must be obvious to you how well placed you are, with no competition to speak of—now that we've routed Jackpot.' He smiled, taking the success for his own.

His self-satisfaction made Kim open then close her mouth. It was no good getting into another wrangle. She was being forced to say yes and would have to put up with it. Ian had described often enough the kind of opportunity for expansion he was looking for. But why did the stranger bearing gifts of gold have to be Con Arlington?

'I would hate Ian to accuse me of looking a gift horse in the mouth,' she told him savagely. She picked up her bag. 'When do I leave?' At least he wouldn't be able to monitor the ingratitude in her heart. He would be miles away in London. There was at least that to be thankful for.

'I thought we'd go out on the Friday afternoon flight and come back early Monday morning. That way it won't cut into the working week and we'll get a full weekend. What's the matter now?' Con's observant eyes had picked up on her tightening lips.

'We?' she croaked.

'Naturally I'm coming along. I want to show you round. Introduce you to Uncle——'

'Surely he could show me round himself?' she retorted in a last-ditch stand, already convinced that whatever Con Arlington wanted he would get.

'I'm sure he'd be delighted—unfortunately he's confined to a bath-chair these days. Abbaye-sur-Lac is the baby that keeps him interested in life.'

'Expensive therapy,' she muttered. He had an answer for everything.

'Yes. But he can afford it.'

An old memory prompted her to say, 'Mother wasn't so lucky.' She rose, pushing back the chair with a fierceness that sent it clattering against the wall, cutting off what he was about to say and reaching the door before he even had time to go through to the next room to settle the bill.

Once outside, she expected some reprimand. The waitress had looked from one to the other with a bemused expression—as if suspecting some lovers' tiff, thought Kim savagely. But Con sauntered over to the car, swinging the keys, very much at ease as usual. Does nothing ruffle those sleek feathers? she scowled, sinking down into the soft leather and avoiding his glance as he checked her seat-belt. The only time she had seen any sign of uncontrolled emotion had been in the alley near the Inns of Court when, presumably, blind lust had momentarily taken over. She shuddered. The kiss in the studio earlier, a kiss engraved on her lips forever, had, after all, been a simple power bid, a demonstration to show how easily he could manipulate her. There had been no feeling involved, no loss of self-control on his part.

Furious with herself, with him, with Ian for landing her in such an impossible situation, and burning with all the old anger at what had happened to her mother five years before, she felt like a living ball of fire. If Con recognised the fact he had the good sense to keep quiet on the drive back, careful not to provoke another outburst. Instead he flicked a switch and the lush sounds of Bruce Springsteen wrapped them in a romantic-sounding haze of melody—at least, it would have been romantic with any other man beside her.

Con left the studio before six after a few words with Ian and some remark about a previous engagement in town, and as the sporty red car disappeared out of sight, Ian turned to Kim with a beaming smile. 'I knew you'd see sense,' he remarked delightedly. 'It's the biggest stroke of luck we've had so far. I knew you were going to be my lucky black cat, Kim.' He tweaked a strand of the black hair, then gave her a sudden hug. 'I didn't realise your mother was so famous. Guess I'm not as well up in the arty-crafty world as I might be.'

'She's not famous. She's dead.' Kim disengaged herself from his embrace and went to the door.

'Hey, Kimmy!' His smile faded. Before she could get out he was by her side. 'Look, I know what you feel about—you know, all that—but you can hardly hold Arlington himself responsible. He's not clairvoyant. And he's not responsible for what people do after they lose a case.'

'I can see his charm has worked on you too.' She paused, then, powered by anger, added icily, 'You should join Laura—she's his number one fan around here, isn't she? If I were you I'd watch her.'

Then, regretting the words as soon as they were out, she slammed out of the studio before she could take them back. Let him stew, she thought bitterly. Laura had the sense to know that Con Arlington was the sort of man to make mincemeat of her. She would have the sense to steer well clear. But Ian would have to work that one out for himself.

*   *   *

The next day passed in a torrent of activity. Striving to bring her work up to date so that she could write off one day on either side of the weekend without any qualms, Kim scarcely had time to brood over the way she had been outmanoeuvred. Laura had managed to book a flight late in the afternoon, giving them time, as she explained to Kim, to do the half-hour's drive to Abbaye-sur-Lac in time for dinner.

'You are lucky, Kim. I'd give anything for it to be me.'

'Do a photography course, then,' snapped Kim, 'and next time it might be you.'

'Do you think I could?' mused Laura, suddenly looking serious. 'I wonder if Ian would give me a job if I did.'

'He might be looking for a photographer after this,' muttered Kim under her breath.

Misunderstanding, Laura gave a little giggle. 'I wonder why.' She began to hum irritatingly.

'"Here Comes the Bride"?' Kim looked up. 'I've never liked Wagner.'

Laura looked blank.

'Though why you should be humming that, Laura, I've no idea. I think the Dead March from *Saul* might be more appropriate. It sums up my attitude to Con Arlington completely.'

'I remember what you said when you first met him,' said Laura.

'So do I. With regret.'

Laura left her then and Kim went home to pack.

She didn't know what sort of clothes would be suitable for a weekend in Abbaye-sur-Lac. She flung any old thing into a small suitcase, then hesitated on the point of tipping them out again with the thought that she might be expected to meet a lot of glamorous people. Con had given no indication what to expect. It was her own fault; she hadn't given him chance.

She fingered a silk dress hanging in the wardrobe, toying with the idea of running an iron over it. For all she knew she would be eating in the kitchen with the other employees. After all, she was going to be there on an assignment. It wasn't a social visit. Still undecided, she ironed the dress and left it hanging up beside the open case. It wouldn't hurt to throw it in at the last minute. If she was consigned to domestic quarters no one would know she had had other expectations.

Then she rang Lizzie in London and put her in the picture. It was a relief to get it off her chest. Lizzie understood how she felt in a way a man like Ian couldn't be expected to—he thought she should forgive and forget. Lizzie was more realistic.

'You'll both have to talk it out if you're to work together. And by the sound of things you'll be bumping into each other often enough in future. And think, Kim, he was younger then, inexperienced. When he knows the full story he might have regrets now about how things turned out.'

'Regrets? You don't know the man, Lizzie. He hasn't had a regret in his life.'

'Well, at least he might accept that he'd have handled the case differently.'

'I doubt that.' Kim refused to be conciliated. 'He's always been interested in coming out on top. Why should he have changed?'

'Play it by ear, then. At least it's going to put some money in the bank!'

Kim drove down to London, suitcase on the back seat, silk dress folded carefully inside together with a pair of shorts and a pair of sunglasses as an after-thought. Lizzie had offered to keep an eye on the car if Kim parked it in the street outside the flat, and, grabbing the parcel she had left for her, she stuffed the key back through the door with a hastily scribbled thank-you note and hailed a cab to take her to Con's chambers as arranged.

The Strand was thick with traffic and she had plenty of time to dwell on what lay ahead. Lizzie was right. She would have to play it by ear, thinking only of her expanding bank account. Implied in all that was a warning not to get into another of those tricky situations where Con Arlington turned her limbs to jelly and common sense flew out of the window. Lips set in a determined line, she paid off the taxi driver and made her way through an alley into the precincts.

By contrast with the rush and bustle of the main throughfare all was tranquillity here, if a little run-down and not as picturesque as it might have been. Where there could have been green lawns in the

courtyards there were only muddy triangles, scored
by the countless footsteps of barristers and clients.

The detailed instructions Con had given her had
irritated her, as did everything else about him. She
had assumed he had been so painstaking because
he regarded her intelligence with contempt. But now
she saw why he had gone to so much trouble. Every
doorway to every building had a board with ten or
twenty names, detailing the occupants of the
chambers within. At least she had made a note of
the name of the house he was in and with that
knowledge it was easy enough to find the right
staircase. From there it was simple to find the door
through which she suddenly feared to step.

She hesitated in the corridor. Distantly the sound
of raised voices came from another room. Then the
decision whether to go in or not was taken from
her, for the door in front of her suddenly flew open
and a man came hurrying out. Another shape followed, blocking the doorway with a ferocious
expression on his face, sending a shiver of apprehension zipping through Kim just to see it. Then
he came forward into the light, and it was Con, and
suddenly the scowl was replaced by the glittering
blue of his smile as he recognised her. He reached
forward and took her suitcase at once, leading her
by the arm into the rooms beyond. She was aston-
ished by the quick-change act, from a man in a
towering rage to this one possessing a glittering
charm. Obviously one of the men was an impostor.
She eyed him suspiciously. It didn't take brains to

decide which one. He was standing right here beside her, looking down at her as if she were the best thing since sliced bread, with an expression that could only be false.

'Good journey?'

'What? Oh, yes. Not bad.'

'I'm sorry, I haven't had time to change yet. You travelling in that?' His glance swept the cotton dress and jacket she wore.

Affronted by his lack of expression, she merely nodded. She would wear what the hell she liked, she thought fiercely; who did he think he was?

His eyes crinkled at the corners. 'You look very chic,' he judged as if he had been able to read her thoughts. 'Very much the professional.'

Not sure whether to be mollified or not, she nearly smiled, remembering only just in time that easy compliments and double-talk were Con's stock in trade. He was obviously putting himself out to appear charming to a prospective employee. But what did she expect, rank insults? That wouldn't be his style.

'When do we leave?' she asked.

'Give me moment. I won't change here. We're a little pushed for time as it is.' Showing her to a chair, he disappeared into another room. As she waited she could hear the distant sound of a typewriter, doors opening and closing, a telephone, voices. This was his habitat. Well, it wasn't luxury. It wasn't a designer dream of the perfect office. In fact it was downright scruffy. Although the paint wasn't actually peeling off the walls it was as near as dammit. Yet Con himself was sleek and obviously well-heeled.

He came back just then and without more ado whisked her downstairs and across a courtyard to where his car was parked. To her relief, once they were clear of the London traffic and spinning along the motorway to the airport, he switched on the radio to a news programme and she was saved the embarrassment of having to find something neutral to say to him. With luck, once at their destination, she would be kept so busy that there would be little time for the intimate contact she so dreaded.

It was a short flight, but even so Con immediately opened his briefcase and took out some papers. 'You don't mind, do you? I don't wish to appear anti-social, but I must check something.' He gave a helpless shrug, burying himself in their contents before she could demur.

Suits me, thought Kim, flicking through a magazine from the rack in front. With no one to talk to, she eventually let her eyes close, lulled into a cosy state on the threshold of sleep by the thrumming of the engines and the rise and fall of surrounding conversations.

A few minutes later she opened her eyes when the plane gave a slight bump as it hit an air-pocket. Her glance flew to Con at once, then she looked again. He was sound asleep! One hand lay on top of the papers he had been scanning, the other hung limply over the arm-rest. His head was slumped against the cushion and there was a beatific expression on his face that almost brought a smile to Kim's lips. There was something so vulnerable about him now the dangerous blue eyes were shielded from sight. His mouth, firmly marked, looked dove-soft, and she had a sudden urge, quickly repressed, to reach out to touch it—remembering how it had felt against her own.

He reminded her of someone else in his dark three-piece pinstripe suit with the top button of the waistcoat undone, his white shirt still pristine, the college tie loosened, and the well-shaped hands disappearing inside deep cuffs with heavy, pale gold links.

Drowsily she tried to remember who he looked like—some film-star, she thought dreamily . . . long, long ago . . . she raked her memory—she must have been ten or so . . . was he French? No, now she remembered. It was the gambler in *The Magnificent Seven*—what was his name? He had gone on to become famous . . . and he had worn the same immaculate, conventional, slightly sinister style of suit, with that chest-hugging dark waistcoat, always perfectly turned out no matter what. Even when he was on the run and was shot down at the end. She remembered crying silently in the darkened cinema as he closed his eyes for the last time. Gangsters, she thought, drifting deeper into sleep. It was Con's job, she supposed, to deal with the underworld. It gave him an unfair allure. Magic of the forbidden. A tough customer under the conventional appearance. A James Bond type, always conscious of the speck of dust on the sleeve, the crease of a trouser, the turn of a cuff. But the eyes were pure Paul Newman.

Something feathered across her cheek; her eyes opened lazily, blinked, then she brought herself abruptly upright as she realised where she was. Con Arlington was leaning over her, one finger having just done to her lips what she had imagined doing to his!

'You looked so sweet I didn't want to wake you, but I don't fancy finishing up at Heathrow again, do you?'

She glanced over his shoulder and saw that the other passengers were already pushing towards the exits.

'Have we landed?' she queried.

'We have indeed.' With a smile he unbuckled her seat-belt.

'I don't remember fastening that.'

'You didn't, I did. Come on. Dinner on the terrace in half an hour.'

Disturbed by his tenderness, she followed him out of the aircraft. His touch as he pushed her on ahead of him made her shudder, recalling her fantasy about him as she had drifted off to sleep. She avoided his glance and let him lead her through the formalities when they disembarked. He knew his way around, and in a few minutes they were sitting in a taxi, speeding along in the unbelievable blue and silver-green that was Provence in early summer.

Kim heaved a sigh of satisfaction. But for the old hatred of the Arlington clan, she could be happy. Very happy indeed. But nothing must let her forget just what sort of debt Con Arlington owed.

CHAPTER FIVE

THE TAXI took the motor route round Montpellier to avoid the worst of the traffic, and after going along the main road for a few miles turned into a lane bordered by pollarded willows. It eventually slowed when it came to an archway set in a high wall smothered in plaited hanks of wistaria and honeysuckle. They were flowering in profusion and the bright colours of wild flowers speckled the long grass on the verge. Kim could see the dark fingers of Lombardy poplars waving from the other side, and guessed that the village of Abbaye-sur-Lac was enclosed within it. Somewhere in the cloudless blue a lark was carolling.

The taxi hiccupped forwards, taking them between the single-carriage width under the arch, coming to rest in a courtyard within the precincts. This would have been the tiny village square, Kim guessed, taking in the stone fountain, the cobblestones studded with wild flowers, the enclosing, shuttered buildings. Despite the silence following Con's fruitless attempts at small talk during the journey from the airport, she couldn't help looking around with interest. It was certainly a picturesque location, much of its charm to do with the air of decay, of rampant, untamed nature running every-

where in multi-coloured riot. She wondered if it
would look so charming once it was tarted up.

A comfortable, two-storeyed house of grey stone
mostly obscured by flowering vines took up one end
of the square, its windows white-shuttered against
the sun, double doors at the top of shallow steps
giving a view into a dark entrance hall. From
outside Kim got an impression of polished floors,
brimming flower bowls, lace door-curtains flurried
by the evening breeze and a flower garden visible
through an open door deep inside.

Con paid off the taxi driver, and when the hoarse
sounds of the cab faded they were enveloped in a
drowsy silence. The place seemed deserted, an oasis
of tranquillity after the turmoil at the airport.

'Let's go and find someone.' Con's eyes were
alight as they met Kim's. Blushing at the unspoken
intimacy of such a look, she followed as with a bag
in each hand he led the way across the square into
the house.

After the dry heat outside it was refreshingly cool
within. Very much at home—when wasn't he?
thought Kim—Con strode down the hall to the
kitchen quarters at the far end. Cries of welcome
greeted the appearance of his head round the door
and he made way for a squat white-aproned woman
of about fifty who came pushing out to take an
inquisitive look at the visitor. Her excited French
took Kim a few moments to unravel but, with
welcome evident on the woman's face, she did her
best to respond as best she could. Picking up their

cases again, Con led the way up a flight of polished wood stairs to a spacious landing with several doors opening off it, one of which he opened, showing her inside.

'I hope you'll be all right here. I think it's got one of the pleasantest views—even though they're all pretty spectacular, as you'll discover.'

Kim stopped herself from exclaiming out loud. He was conceited enough, but he was right: the view was heavenly. They stood side by side at the window drinking it in in silence.

As she had guessed, the inner door glimpsed from the entrance did give on to a flower garden. It was bounded by more grey stone, tile-capped in red, and even here it was untamed, clipped just here and there to enable the flowers to blossom. Beyond that was what looked like a stretch of woodland, then a hill of silver-green olive trees, with now and then a hint of grey outcrop, a building, a bridge.

'Is there a river?' Unable to help herself, Kim broke the silence first.

'Yes, you can get a glimpse of it through the trees there. It runs right through the property, and there's an eighteenth-century canal bordered by ornamental yews running from it. Look, it's a line of darker green over there.' Con pointed into the distance and she leaned closer to follow his glance, the movement bringing her into sudden contact with his shoulder. She sprang back as if she had been electrocuted, gasping, 'Sorry!' then colouring violently at the giveaway reaction.

He gave a laugh, eyebrows lifting in sardonic amusement. 'It's all right, you didn't do any damage.' He added as an afterthought, 'Not physically, at least.'

Kim's confusion deepened. He made her feel as clumsy as a ten-ton elephant, his presence so overpowering he seemed to fill the room, making her feel as if she were about to bump into things even when she wasn't. There just wasn't room for the two of them in it. It was no mystery why she felt so hemmed in when Con was near. She looked at him with an expression that tried to tell him it was time to leave. To her surprise he picked it up at once.

'OK, later, hm?' He raised an eyebrow, his blue glance washing over her. 'I want to change before dinner and I'm sure you do too,' he said. 'There's a shower through here.' He moved swiftly to the white door she had assumed was a cupboard and opened it with a flourish to reveal a quite spacious bathroom suite. 'And anything else you want,' he turned, eyes crinkling, 'just call my name.'

'Literally?'

'Yes. I'm across the corridor.' He smiled in a manner Kim could only describe as suggestive, and she hurried over to her suitcase, bending her head behind a curtain of hair to hide her confusion, trusting he would take the hint and leave.

After the door closed she flopped down on to the bed. It was heaven here, but Con was like a time-bomb waiting to go off. He terrified her. She had no idea how to handle him. An aloof distance seemed the best approach. But would he allow that? Lizzie had suggested talking as a way of resolving their differences, but talk wasn't going to do any good. It couldn't change the past. And anyway, he was only interested in getting her to fit in with his preconceived ideas. And that wasn't what she wanted in any relationship, friendly or...she shuddered...friendly, or even one that was something more.

'Something more?' She got up and stood beside the window. There could never be anything more with Con Arlington. He was the enemy, had always been, would always be. She must never forget that.

The kiss, a fragment of time detached from its proper place in the past, danced before her eyes.

While the reverberations of a dinner gong were still resounding throughout the house there was a light knock on Kim's door. Showered and wearing a magenta silk blouse with matching flowered skirt, she bit back her fears and went to answer it. Con had changed. For a split second she felt her jaw drop a little. After the dark, ever-so-correct business suit, he was now wearing a pale silky-looking dinner jacket and matching trousers, and with his dark hair and gold tan enhanced by this pale attire he looked rakish, foreign and dangerously attractive.

He proffered his arm. 'Shall we go down?'

Not daring to take it, she walked on in front, keeping as much space between them as she could.

After one swift almost imperceptible lift of his head Con let her take the lead, only going in front when they reached the bottom of the stairs.

'Don't be worried by Uncle David. He's just a crazy old man.' He said it affectionately, but Kim wondered what lay ahead.

In fact there was no need for anxiety. True to family tradition, this other member of the Arlington clan was charm itself. Perhaps in his seventies, though illness could have made him look older, he had the same blue eyes as Con Arlington, though the hair was a shock of white sweeping eccentrically to his shoulders. Sitting in a bath-chair near the open french windows of the sitting-room, he was formally dressed in a beige cotton jacket, at his throat a flamboyant black bow like a Spanish grandee and, almost the first thing Kim noticed, a magnificent opal ring on the right hand he extended to her. As she took it he drew hers down to him so that he could plant a kiss on the back of it.

'Charming, quite charming,' he murmured, assessing Kim thoughtfully, then giving his nephew a quick lift of his eyebrows as a sign of approval.

There was no time to say anything other than to remark on the journey, for at that moment a group sauntered in from the terrace, talking casually and obviously well acquainted with each other.

'This is my doctor, my architect, his beautiful assistant Mariette, and the assorted wives etc. of the first two.' He waved a hand as if to disclaim any lack of politeness. 'I leave you to render names,

Conan.' He pronounced it Co-nan, formal and correct. Watching him now, controlling the conversation from his bath-chair, Kim was struck by the mixture of informality and correctness in the household. A maid entered, confirming this impression, wearing a uniform of black dress and pretty white lace cap and apron, yet apparently carrying on a teasing backchat with her employer which was anything but formal. It seemed like an Arlington trait, this wilful establishment of the way things should be and to hell with what anybody else expected.

'I'm Mariette,' said a voice at her shoulder. 'Glad to meet you. It will be so nice to have another woman around. I understand you'll be working here for some time.'

'I don't know yet,' Kim replied, ignoring the way Con suddenly came to attention beside her.

'I do hope so.' Mariette, tiny, blonde, chic, gave her a friendly smile.

Con quickly introduced Kim to the doctor's wife and to the architect, Raoul, a young newly-wed, and his wife Lulu, and went to get her an aperitif.

Then she turned, expecting to greet the final member of the group, but, coming in last from the terrace, the woman ignored Kim and instead sauntered over to pour herself some Perrier, only turning when Con came up beside her. She said something in rapid French, throwing back her red head to reveal a long white throat. Con laughed, reaching across her for a glass, turning to listen to what else she was saying as he mixed the drinks.

They seemed to stand together for ages, ignoring the rest of the gathering, Kim's drink still in his hand, the woman, presumably one of the daughters alluded to already, resting one hand lightly on Con's sleeve as she talked. It was a gesture that Kim found wholly irritating.

She was pleased when they all moved outside again, one of the maids manoeuvering David Arlington's bath-chair, and everyone else seating themselves informally around a large table beneath a peach tree.

Compared to England the weather was glorious, and Kim rested her elbows on the table, listening to the mixture of French and English flying back and forth, trying to tune in to what was being said.

It was talk mainly concerning mutual friends. Con seemed to know them all. He fitted in as if he lived here all the time, and she wondered how often he made the short flight from England. Often enough, by the look of things. She glanced again at the redhead, whose name, she gathered, was Lisette. She had placed herself right next to Con, buttonholing him into a semi-private conversation that excluded everyone else. Con didn't seem to mind in the least. Kim turned away. It was nothing to her. It just made her feel sick to see him carrying on as if he had never kissed her, never tried to make her feel he was interested. Probably he was exactly the same with every woman he met—his type usually couldn't help themselves.

She tried to follow some story Raoul was telling about one of the local farmers, finding that her school French was only just about adequate to get the gist. It was annoying. She found herself in the position of laughing when everyone else did, not really understanding the joke. Then Con caught her eye in a look of secret complicity as if he understood. He held her glance for a split second too long for it to be accidental. She felt her chin rise. How could he? Putting out meaningful looks to one woman while chatting up another! Lisette hadn't noticed, being too wrapped up in the effect she was having to pay much attention.

From then on Kim deliberately avoided Con's glance, pretending an avid interest in what everyone else was talking about, and it was only when the meal was drawing to a conclusion and the maid came out bearing a huge silver coffee pot that a surreptitious glance at Con showed that he had managed to tear himself away from Lisette at last.

He came to sit in the vacant chair beside her when the doctor's wife got up. She could feel his arm resting across the back of her own. 'Coping with the language?'

'Well enough.' She avoided his glance, refusing to appear friendly just because he had condescended to talk to her.

'As far as the job goes it doesn't matter at all,' he told her. 'But if you're stuck you know I'm available.' He studied her closely. 'You do know that, don't you?'

'What?' Her head jerked round.

'That I'm available.'

'So, evidently, does Lisette,' she remarked, picking up her empty wineglass and putting it down again.

'Then she'd be wrong, wouldn't she?'

'Really?' Kim refused to bend.

'Yes, really.'

'I can't see why you're telling me this.' She glanced away as if looking for an escape.

'Go on, Kim, I credit you with some imagination.' He was not talking so quietly no one else could have heard even if they had wanted to. But they didn't want to; they were all engrossed in their own conversations. More wine was brought out. The coffee urn was refilled and a cheese board was still circulating. Someone lit up a cigar and the smoke drifted across the lawn, its scent blending aromatically with that of peach blossom.

'I have plenty of imagination, actually,' she replied, after a pause, keeping her voice low, 'not that there's much need where you're concerned.'

He laughed softly. 'I'm sure I still have a few surprises up my sleeve.'

'In that case I hope you'll keep them for those who'll appreciate them,' she muttered angrily in return.

'And don't you think you would—once you knew what they were?' he teased.

'I know I wouldn't.'

'Then your imagination is limited after all. I guess I shall have to consider doing something about that.'

'Do you have an answer for everything, Mr Arlington?'

'Mister again, am I? What a pity. I thought we were beginning to get on a more friendly footing.'

'As I've already told you, as far as I'm concerned this is strictly business.'

'This is?' His eyes lazed over her flushed face, swept over the laden table with its bulging bowls and carafes. 'I would have hoped you would see this as a pleasant interlude before we start work tomorrow morning.'

'Work, Mr Arlington, yes. I wouldn't even be here if it weren't for work.'

'No, I can see that—heaven knows how I would have persuaded you if you hadn't been a dab hand with a drawing-pencil!'

'You wouldn't have. You know you only got me here because of Ian. You counted on the fact that I wouldn't want to let him down.'

'I did rather,' he admitted.

'And you even have the gall to admit it!' she snapped back.

'Darling,' he murmured, 'I also have the gall, if that's how you want to put it, to admit to being willing to stoop to practically anything to have you by my side.' His eyes were suddenly lustreless, as if he were calculating the effect of such a declaration.

Kim left him in no doubt. 'Look, cut it out. Of any man on earth, you're the last I would ever get involved with.'

He picked up her hand as it lay on the tablecloth and slowly, almost absent-mindedly, placed his lips in a kiss on the back of it. 'When you fly home on Monday I hope you'll have changed your mind.'

'No way!'

He placed her hand back on the cloth. 'We'll see, Kim, my sweet, we shall see.'

Then he got up and strolled over towards the house for something. Relieved to see him go, she had no chance to recover before Lisette was sliding into the vacated seat.

Unexpectedly she spoke fluent English. 'I see you get on well with darling Con,' she smiled with a flash of even white teeth. Her eyes moved coolly over Kim's still flustered expression. 'He's a gorgeous guy, isn't he? Everyone's mad about him, of course. It's inclined to make him behave rather naughtily! Still, one always forgives him, he's such a darling!' She patted Kim on the arm. 'Don't worry, he doesn't take *anyone* seriously!' Then she got up and swayed languidly towards the house.

Kim watched her go. The woman's patronising attitude was almost as annoying as Con's assumption that he could make her change her mind about him! What a pair! They thoroughly deserved each other! She remembered the night in the pub when she had first set eyes on him. His companion then had been a redhead too. Well, as Laura had said, 'That lets me out.'

Furious with herself for even harbouring such thoughts, she was still honest enough to recognise his attraction and to know that she felt annoyed to discover that Lisette regarded him as her own personal property. But then perhaps he was. By the deliberate way Lisette had been ignoring Kim all evening until just now it was obvious she saw Kim's presence as some kind of threat.

Nothing could be less likely, thought Kim ruefully. He was as safe as houses as far as she was concerned. In fact it was a relief to find he was booked; it would make her own resolution to avoid him all the easier.

He came out of the house just as Lisette reached the terrace. Obviously having gone in search of him, she now sauntered back by his side, but he came straight over to Kim, touching her on the shoulder. 'Kim, I'm sure you hate sitting around when you're here to work.' He paused long enough for her to wonder what was coming next, and he went on, 'So it might be a good idea to take the opportunity to have a look over part of the grounds now.'

He took her firmly by the arm and urged her to get up. She rose before she could think up an excuse. Everybody else, apart from Lisette, of course, was beginning to drift over to the terrace to catch the last rays of the sun. 'I'm going to show you around a little bit before it gets too dark,' Con told her. 'There's a pleasant walk from the house to the water gardens.'

Just as Kim was wondering how she could get out of it Lisette, overhearing, broke in with an exclamation. 'Lovely! I haven't been up there since——' she broke off and gave Con a coy glance, 'oh, since you know when, darling!' Before he could answer she turned, and calling to everyone on the terrace, invited them along too.

Kim observed Con's flicker of annoyance with satisfaction. So he could be outmanoeuvred! It would be interesting to see how he reacted.

Raoul and his wife got up, reluctantly followed by Mariette, and everyone dutifully trooped down the steps towards them. There was an ironic smile on Mariette's face as she strolled over to where Kim was standing. Lisette was already hanging on to Con's arm as he led the way.

'They'll be going home soon. Lisette's car's in the garage, so she had to come over with her people. The doctor likes his early nights,' she told Kim in a casual manner.

'She can stay as long as she likes!' replied Kim, catching Mariette's eye and pulling a little face. 'I'm sure Con will jump at the opportunity of driving her!'

The Frenchwoman gave a laugh. 'Maybe he won't! Don't count on it!' Then she gave Kim a sidelong glance. 'We'll get on all right, you and I, eh?'

Kim returned her smile. 'I hope so. I can do with an ally out here.'

'You have an even more beautiful man at home, *n'est-ce pas*?' Mariette shook her head as if it was difficult to believe. 'You must bring him over some time.'

Kim laughed. 'It's not quite like that.' She let the matter drop then and they walked on after the others to where a narrow path, wide enough for two, led through a rose garden, then began to drop steeply through banks of rhododendrons towards the river bank.

Con handed everyone down the steps at the top, but when he came to Kim, who was bringing up the rear, he didn't let her hand go as she jumped the last step, but hung on to it, forcing her to walk by his side down the narrow path, their bodies brushing as they avoided overhanging branches on either side. Ahead, Lisette swivelled to watch, but the path was too narrow for her to make her way back to them. Raoul and Lulu urged her onwards.

Kim dragged her feet to let the others get on ahead, then she turned to her companion. 'Listen to me, Con. I don't know what your relationship with Lisette is, but if you're using me to make her jealous you can stop right now!' she exploded.

He looked at her in astonishment, his blue eyes suddenly icy. 'You have a child's mind in a woman's body, dear Kim, if that's what you think. At the risk of sounding conceited, do you seriously imagine I need to try to make anyone jealous?' His lip curled. 'There's only one reason for wanting to walk along this rather romantic river path with you—and it's this.'

Before she could turn he pulled her roughly into his arms, both hands travelling at the same time over her hips so that she was instantly aware of how aroused he was already. With one hand holding her tight and the other snaking rapidly up her spine to the back of her neck to tilt her head, she was effectively trapped. His lips came down quickly, crushing hers, then, as she opened her mouth to cry out, his own opened, pressuring alternately soft, then hard as he succumbed to the urgency of his desire.

She heard a small groan released deep inside her throat as his tongue began to play against her own, sending shivers of unexpected pleasure coursing through her body. She wanted to struggle free, but her limbs refused to obey and for a moment they clung to each other, undulating in a harmony of shared need on the path, until with a little shock, Kim remembered their companions and her fixed opinion of Con Arlington. It sent her pushing back as she tried to resist the impulse to yield, struggling a little to free herself, disconcerted to find he was too strong and too determined to let her go at once, and every little touch of his hands over her body made her resistance weaken in an alarming fashion. She was actually enjoying the experience! His body was so fit and firm, his touch so exciting he was making her give in already!

Despite her best intentions she found herself slackening against him, allowing him to support her weight, her head tilting as his hardness arched her over with one hand supporting her in the small of the back as the other explored her breasts, dipping inside the low neckline of her blouse to cradle a smooth mound in his warm grasp.

She couldn't resist him, but her initial panic at finding herself so helpless abated when she realised the others were still within earshot. She could hear their voices, now near, now far, through the canopy of trees. Soon they would realise Con was missing and come back for him. Lisette wouldn't let him stay out of sight too long.

As if realising this himself, Con slowly brought his movements to a stop, dragging his dark head from where it bent over her, eyes that had been closed in concentration flickering open to lick over her face with a glitter of blue that showed he knew the situation was impossible even if he guessed he could override her resistance, given the chance.

It was that look more than anything else that brought Kim back to reality. She knew he had seen every nuance of emotion on her face, every last sign of wanton desire before she could switch it off, and now his expression had changed, triumph taking over from the supplications of a rampant desire, and he gave a soft, knowing laugh.

'I could make quite a meal of you, darling, and I do believe you could do the same with me!' He gave a soft chuckle as he reminded her of words she had used before. 'Far better than eating poison, don't you agree?'

She shook her head, her eyes wild as she recalled the need to resist. But he merely murmured, 'You're pretending. We both know what we feel—more's the pity we're not alone.'

He bent quickly and gave her lips a little nip with his sharp teeth, dragging her briefly up against him, then turning and, holding her by his side, walked her further along the path after the others, gripping her tightly to him all the time so that he was half carrying her as her legs seemed to buckle. She could feel one hand firmly clamped beneath her breast so that even as they walked she was left in no doubt of the sensuality of his caress as his fingers edged inside her blouse.

She was too confused to put up much resistance. Her feelings warred against her mind. Knowing who he was, she had been convinced until now that the last thing she wanted was any deepening of the contact between them, yet here she was, totally swept off her feet by a kiss!

As her head tilted, trees seemed to swim above, shutting out the sunlight, locking them both in a strange green world of their own, and with a small groan Con lifted her face to his for the last time as they reached the turn in the path that would bring them into full view of everyone else. She could already hear the others calling for them as his lips ravaged hers in a brief, possessive taking. Then she was sliding free and he moved away. Sunlight broke through the screening branches, and the others turned in the clearing to watch them emerge from the path.

Con called across even before he reached them. 'We'll go as far as the boathouse, shall we?' His voice was firm, unruffled, and Kim marvelled at his self-possession. Her own limbs were shaking so violently she had to make a definite effort to appear calm, especially when Lisette, with a suspicious look at her, stalked over to Con and took him possessively by the arm.

Everyone but Lisette turned to go on with murmurs of agreement. Kim crossed the clearing just as Lisette reached up to whisper something in his ear. She couldn't hear what she said to him, but he put a hand in the small of her back and pushed her on ahead. Pulling herself together, Kim carried on walking, reaching the others before Con could turn. Let him walk behind with Lisette, she thought wildly. What had just happened must never happen again. Her mind a blank, she moved as if in a dream. Nothing seemed real.

She avoided Con after that. It was easy enough to make sure she was talking to one or the other of the group. Unwittingly Lisette aided her, hanging on to Con's arm whenever she got the opportunity.

They spent a while beside the boathouse, admiring the view of the lily-covered lake and listening to Con describing David Arlington's plans for the water gardens. Then, before it got dark, they wended their way back along the river bank, turning on to the overgrown path down which they had just come.

Kim tried to wipe all expression from her face as they passed the place where Con, not to say she herself, had lost control. Her emotions were still in turmoil. It was all so out of character. She had never acted like this before. It was as if suddenly no rules existed to tell her how to behave. She shivered at the thought of what might have happened if the others hadn't been within earshot and Con had insisted on having his own way. The thought made her tremble with a mixture of longing and fear. The weekend was fraught with more danger than she had anticipated when she had agreed to come. Never before had she felt so incapable of controlling her own longings.

She could sense Con's presence behind her now and couldn't help wondering what thoughts were going through his mind. Prickles of apprehension crawled rapidly up the back of her spine as they passed the very spot where he had taken her in his arms.

How was she going to keep him at a distance all weekend—when in reality she wanted to do no such thing? With a man like him a simple 'no' surely wouldn't work; instead it would be more like a challenge. He was used to fighting for what he wanted, practising his powers of persuasion. And he was used to winning too. Talking to him wouldn't work either, for the same reason—he would turn all her arguments upside down. Instinctively she knew he would like nothing better than to talk her into bed, using sheer force of logic. It would be a game to him, a game at which he was supreme master.

She caught up with Mariette when they reached the steps. 'Tomorrow?' she asked. 'You will be around, I hope?'

'Naturally.'

'And Sunday?'

'I do have some time off, you know. Why?' Kim's strained expression must have been obvious. Mariette was looking at her rather oddly.

'Nothing. I just wondered... It's all sort of strange for me here.' Kim turned away. The dangerous times would be when Mariette had gone and work was over. Her head spun with the effort of trying to solve the problem. She turned to see Con climbing the steps towards them.

He came over to them. 'The others are leaving. Come in for a nightcap, Mariette. I want to talk about our schedule for tomorrow.'

Feeling that he must have read her thoughts and somehow overheard what she was saying to Mariette, Kim imagined he was already plotting to block her only avenue of escape as she followed them inside. She wondered if Mariette understood she had tentatively been cast in the role of chaperon.

Goodbyes were already being said, and Lisette, much to Kim's surprise, left with only the barest brushing of Con's lips with her own.

When they got inside, Con's uncle David was nowhere to be seen, but a light had been left on in the drawing-room shedding an intimate glow over the sofa. It was like a stage set for seduction. Not trusting herself, Kim deliberately chose one of the seats as far away from the sofa as possible, and to her relief Mariette flung herself down in the middle so that it looked natural for Kim to avoid it.

'I'll come in about ten tomorrow, if that's all right with you and Kim,' she said. 'I have to be in Montpellier by late afternoon.' Her glance swung to Kim's anxious face. 'Though I suppose I can stay on a little longer if you want me to.'

'We'll see how things go,' Con told her. 'I'm going to persuade Kim to put on her walking shoes.' He turned to her. 'I think you should walk the estate this weekend so that you can get an idea of its scope. You can pick out the places you'll want to sketch while we talk to the builders.' His tone was matter-of-fact. 'How does that suit you?' He lifted a brow. It was as if the kiss on the path had been a dream. There was no sign on his face that they had done anything more intimate than shake hands. She flinched from his gaze, jerking her head up and down in agreement.

'As long as I can get some initial sketches done. I don't want to waste my time this weekend.' Her eyes were brimming with emotions held fiercely in check. He must have been able to tell something was wrong, because his glance, covering hers as she spoke, swivelled back again and the blue eyes pierced her expression as if he was surprised to read what was so obviously in it.

'We'll talk in a minute,' he told her curtly.

'I'm off, then, if tomorrow's settled.' Mariette rose to her feet and Kim watched her leave as if her lifeline were being cut.

While Con was showing Mariette to the door fear made Kim take the initiative and sent her running lightly up the stairs behind his back, only feeling safe when she was inside her room with the key firmly turned in the lock.

It wasn't sophisticated to act in this way. But she felt so inexperienced faced with a man like Con. He was an expert player in the game of love and must be able to tell she was out of her depth. He was a marauder, a barbarian, taking whoever he wanted with no regard for feelings. No appeal to his better nature would succeed because he wouldn't understand. So she had to take this extreme action, she told herself—she had to protect herself, finding no other protection at Abbaye-sur-Lac.

It wasn't long before she heard footsteps outside her door. She was sitting bolt upright in bed and put a hand up to the neck of her cotton nightie as if he were already in the room ready to rip it from her heated body.

'Kim?' The door handle turned. 'Kim, have you locked the door?'

'I'm tired. I want to go to sleep.'

There was an answering laugh, soft and knowing. 'Never will locked doors keep us two apart, my love.' He made it sound like a line from a piece of poetry, not a threat.

Safe on the other side, she shivered. Then there came an unexpected 'Sleep well!' and quite suddenly his footsteps receded.

She had half expected him to batter down the door. It was a relief when she heard the gentle slam of the one opposite. Then silence fell.

CHAPTER SIX

KIM hadn't realised that building work was already going on at Abbaye, and she awoke to the sound of a concrete-mixer buzzing away in the distance like an irate bluebottle.

She lay there in bed for a few minutes going over the events of the previous day. Her locked door now seemed melodramatic, a gesture born of an overheated imagination and too much strong wine. To be frightened that she wouldn't be able to keep a man at bay seemed silly, and she smiled to herself. She wasn't such an idiot that she couldn't say no—and no to a man like Con Arlington should be the easiest thing in the world, with all the pain he had caused in the past as a young Daniel of a barrister!

Feeling cheerful and self-confident and keen to get started, she quickly showered, pulled on a pair of jeans and a short-sleeved shirt, then, grabbing her cameras and a sketch-book, went downstairs. There was no sign of Con, and wondering where he was, she made her way towards the kitchens. The housekeeper was already bustling into the hallway and she sent Kim outside to sit on the terrace at a table already freshly laid for one.

Surprised that Con must already have breakfasted, despite the fact that it was still early, she rapidly consumed a delicious breakfast of home-made croissants and a large milky bowl of French coffee. She had read *Paris-Match* twice before a shadow fell over the page she held open, and she looked up with a start, having been unaware of someone watching her and knowing even before she saw him who it was.

'Everyone looking after you properly?' Con's voice honeyed over her with its hint of intimacy beneath the polite concern. It sent a shock spiral-ling through her, as if she had forgotten its sound and had to re-learn its nuances all over again. But his manner plainly set the tone for the day, and he looked cool and efficient in a bright blue work-shirt and a pair of old jeans. His hair gleamed like a raven's wing. Kim felt her jaw drop a little. It was unfair that, even dressed like this, he managed to look devastating. It was immoral for a man to look so desirable! But he had evidently chosen his gear for practicality rather than to impress. Everything about him told her so. He held a thick file in one hand and had obviously been at work already. As he came close, a brief picture of what the body be-neath the clothes was like flashed through her mind and she found herself gripping the edges of her magazine as if something so flimsy could protect her from the desires he instantly aroused. Her self-confidence had drained instantly.

'Let's go,' he said when he noticed her empty cup.

Kim stood up, but, contrary to his words, he didn't move away. Instead he seemed to freeze, then very slowly he bent the heavy, dark head towards her and, while she was still unsure what he was going to do, he placed a slow, warm kiss upon her lips. Then he lifted his head, sea-blue eyes sparkling into hers. 'Good morning angel. You look heavenly in that work-shirt. I've never liked frills and flounces.'

'Con——' she gulped, putting out a hand as he turned to go.

He swung back, his eyes skimming all the way up her body again and coming to rest with a sort of caress on her worried face. 'What is it?' he asked.

'Leave me alone,' she muttered, dropping her glance. 'Just leave me alone, will you?'

'Which part of you is talking?'

'All of me,' she lied. 'I'll never forgive you. It only makes things worse to have you——' she looked hurriedly away, 'to have you touching me the way you do.'

'Even a little good-morning kiss?'

She nodded. Little, he called it! She was rocked to her very soul by that brief magic. Couldn't he see that? Then she hoped he couldn't, for he would undoubtedly take it as carte blanche to storm her defences.

'Do you think I can meekly accept what you say? For one thing, I simply don't believe you, and for another——' he paused and ran a hand through the glossy hair, rumpling it after it had been so neat.

He reached out and gently unbunched both her fists. 'I told you last night, Kim, locked doors won't stop us. And you know it. That's why you're trying to talk yourself out of it now.'

'There's nothing to talk my way out of,' she said in a choking voice, furious with herself for being so easily read. 'You seem to forget I know a hell of a lot more about you than I would have guessed if we'd only just met!'

'But we *have* only just met.'

'Don't play with words. If I didn't actually set eyes on you five years ago I got a very good idea of what type you were. There's only one possible opinion to have about a man like you.'

'Is there? Is there really?' His lips twisted. 'I would suggest, dear Miss Wetherby, that your vehemence now is due in large measure to the fact that you've found more than one possible opinion, and the resulting confusion——' he paused, 'hell, Kim, it makes you look so very sweet!'

'Stop it! Stop being so patronising and—and——' she searched her mind for something really cutting to call him, but could only add lamely, 'and pompous!'

He laughed. 'Sorry—I do lapse a bit sometimes. It's the job. Very useful to be pompous in court sometimes.' His eyes crinkled. 'I'll try to be a little more racy in future.'

'Don't try on my account!' she sparked back. 'I hate you and I always shall!'

'So you say. But, rather than putting me off, it makes me want to try my hand at persuading you to think again. As I've said, I'm sure I can, given the time.'

'You're not going to get the time. I'm here to work,' she replied, drawing herself up. Whatever she said to him he always seemed to be there, blocking her escape and bringing her back to his own argument. With one haughty look drawn from somewhere out of her repertoire, she picked up her drawing materials, slung the camera over one shoulder and marched to the edge of the terrace. 'Can we go? Or are we going to stand here all day, bandying words?'

'Ma'am,' he gave a mock bow, 'to the woods!'

Despite the suggestiveness of this, there was little danger, as she soon discovered, for they were accompanied every step of the way not only by Mariette and Raoul but by a whole army of workmen too. If she had known all this beforehand she could have saved face and avoided their futile breakfast-time wrangle. Still, she thought, at least Con knows where he stands. And, she realised with a shudder, so did she!

A little army of them wandered all over the village that day. The sun blazed hotly down from a cloudless sky and but for the emotional clouds it could have been paradise.

It soon dawned on Kim that Con had been so positive about arranging her visit this weekend because he had known already that he was going to have to come over himself to make a thorough inspection of the renovations so far. It was convenient for him that she was present too. That hadn't been the point of his own visit here at all. He was simply killing two birds with one stone—checking the work that had been carried out, and instructing her on the sort of thing he wanted from Image Design at the same time. Seeing him in charge of the group of men and with Mariette following beside him, making detailed notes, she began to see that she was only a very small cog in the Arlington machine after all.

As the day went on the feeling increased. How she could ever have imagined differently was simply due to Con's predatory approaches. His interest in her was merely that he liked the idea of a romantic diversion on the side. Even a workaholic like Con Arlington must take time off.

She mentioned his apparent dedication to work to Mariette when they stopped for a picnic lunch on the far side of the lake. They had both taken off their sandals and were paddling in the shallows.

'When does he have time off?' asked Kim. 'He's been in court all week, and now this!'

'He's not over here every weekend. He'll fly out maybe once a month. I think, given the choice, he'd be here all the time. But his family committed him to the law years ago, so that's what he does. I expect he's very good too!'

'Oh, very,' replied Kim faintly.

They rejoined the others then and after a lavish picnic continued their perambulation round the site. They must have walked miles, for by the time Kim returned to the house about six o'clock she felt pleasantly tired with the sort of languor that comes from hot sun and plenty of exercise.

Con had gone over to the office on the other side of the square with Mariette and Raoul, so Kim took the opportunity to have a leisurely shower. It entered her head that the evening might herald renewed dangers if she and Con were to be alone together. But then she thought of his uncle and the presence of other people in the house. It wasn't as if they would be on a desert island!

Putting all these thoughts aside, she showered, then, naked in the heat, went over to the bed and opened up the parcel Lizzie had left for her at the flat in London.

As a final-year fashion student, a job with one of the major fashion houses already lined up, Lizzie often persuaded Kim try out her latest designs. 'You're doing me a favour,' she had insisted when Kim had hesitated over borrowing a fragile-looking evening dress not so long ago. 'I want my designs to be wearable. Treat them rough—I need to know what they'll stand up to.'

Now Kim shook out the things Lizzie had packed up before she came away. She hadn't expected to have time to wear anything special, and, unsure when she set off whether she was to stay as a guest or an employee, had only brought the silk dress

with her. It wouldn't do any harm to see if there
was anything more suitable for this evening in
Lizzie's bundle. Silk for one of the lowly workers
would surely be overdoing it. Con's dislike of what
he called 'frills and flounces' had nothing to do
with it.

She shook out the first garment that tumbled out.
It was pure white cotton lace. She held it up to take
a good look. It was a plain slip of a dress, craftily
cut to need no zips or buttons. Curious to see how
it hung, she slipped it over her head. Looking down,
she realised it certainly required underwear—her
skin was clearly visible through the tiny holes in the
patterned lace—but after a sweltering day the cool
cotton was heavenly to wear.

She moved about in it. It was lovely, but totally
unsuitable.

Just then she heard a sound behind her and,
turning her head, she froze in surprise.

Con was standing in the doorway, a stunned
expression on his face. Their eyes met in one wild,
shared explosion of feeling.

Con was the first to recover. 'My apologies, I
didn't expect...' He shrugged as if disclaiming responsibility for Kim's embarrassment. 'The door
wasn't locked.'

His words whipped up an immediate response.
'You mean that gives you the right to go barging
into other people's rooms?'

'No—yes...' He gave a lazy smile, now fully re-
covered. 'I mean, only sometimes—but I shall im-

prove my record if this is what I've been missing. I don't know what that thing is you're wearing, but if you intend to wear it in public warn me beforehand and I'll get the Chief of Police to bring out the riot squad. You look utterly bewitching!' He pretended to flatten himself against the door. 'I hope you intend to keep your distance?'

Kim drew herself up, momentarily forgetting that every ripple of her body was visible beneath the fine lace. 'I have no intention of doing anything else.'

'Really?' Evidently taking her remark as a challenge, he sauntered into the middle of the room after rather ominously pressing the door closed behind him, saying, 'I wonder how amenable to persuasion you are.'

'Get out!' She backed, stumbling against a corner of the bed. 'I've already told you to keep away from me!'

He held both hands out to the sides like someone trying to show they were unarmed. 'I won't come a step nearer—promise. I just wanted to ask you where you'd like to dine this evening. Looking at you now there's only one answer.'

Thinking he meant some nearby restaurant, she lifted her eyebrows.

'Bed,' he replied succinctly. 'A large four-poster for preference.'

'Con, please!' she exclaimed, her resolution weakened by the constant effort of having to fight her own blazing desires as well as his own, 'I can't play your games. I'm not like the women you know. Like Lisette and——' She meant the redhead she had seen him with in the London pub but didn't want to admit she had noticed her. 'I'm not the type to jump into bed with an employer, with anyone, when there's no real feeling. In your world you think of this sort of thing as fun, but I'm not like that. I'm really not. Real feelings come into it as well.'

She raised a pale face, her hair still damp from the shower, standing out in little elf-locks reaching past her shoulders. In the slim white tube of a dress she looked like a wild-eyed waif. Con took a step forward, then seemed to remember his promise, surprising himself by suddenly wanting to behave like a gentleman.

'No feeling?' he asked hoarsely. 'Who says there's no feeling?'

'You know there isn't. I'm a challenge to you just as any woman is, and my feelings are——'

'Confused?'

'No!' She lifted her head, recalling vividly the one very good reason she had for hating him. 'They're all too clear!'

'If this is a ploy, Kim, let me remind you, time is on my side.' Con gave her a lopsided smile, disguising his own raging confusion. Of course she wanted him, he thought wildly, but for some reason she wouldn't even admit it to herself.

To Kim it seemed plain that he believed if he waited long enough she would fall into his bed without a struggle. She had to put him straight. 'I

can never, ever forgive you. I know it's five years
ago, but what you did will last forever and there
can be no forgiving. I admit you're an attractive
guy—when you turn on the charm full blast
anybody would find it difficult to resist. But there's
too much between us from the past to make me
want to forgive you—ever. You see, I know what
you can be like. I know how cold, how heartless,
how destructive you can be. You destroyed the most
precious person in my life, and for that I shall never
forgive you!' She gulped. 'I was weak yesterday
evening when I allowed you to kiss me, but we both
know there was no real feeling there, neither from
you nor from me. I felt only a fleeting desire for a
handsome man with a——' She hesitated.

'Yes?'

She lifted a dismissive shoulder and tried to give
a laugh that would put him in his place. 'With an
impressive physique.' To say it aloud like that
seemed to put it in perspective. What did it matter
that she disowned the rampant longings shaking her
soul? It was a fever which would quickly abate if
she didn't commit the folly of nurturing it. Convinced of this, she found the strength to move over
to the parcel of clothes lying on the bed. 'Now if
you wouldn't mind I'd like to slip into something
a little more suitable.'

'I can't imagine what that might be. That thing
seems eminently suitable to me.' Con seemed dazed
and appeared to ignore what she had just told him,

instead letting his eyes dwell on her like a man mes-
merised by some fantastic apparition.

When she turned with a cutting glance he came
to his senses. For a second they simply looked at
each other, their eyes meeting in an almost tangible
encounter. Kim felt it was a moment of no return.
He would do as she said, falling for her bluff, really
believing she could never give in—when she wasn't
even sure of that herself—or he would pressure just
that little bit more, sending her house of cards tum-
bling. If the latter she wouldn't dare imagine the
consequences.

But after a breath-stopping pause he gave a small
shrug, letting his glance trail regretfully over her
near-naked form in its tantalising sheath before
backing towards the door.

When he reached it he stopped, his hand on the
knob, his eyes holding her prisoner in their bright
blue gaze, and when he spoke his voice was rough
with suppressed emotion. 'I promise you, Kim,' he
husked, 'you're going to wear that scrap of heaven
in bed for me one night. We'll dine like royalty in
an orgy of pleasure before we're through. And
that's a promise.' Then the door closed and he was
gone.

More than if he had ravished her body, Kim felt
shaken to the foundations of her being. Con had
ravished her soul in one sentence, and if he had
stayed she would have been his. But how could she
want this man of all men after what he had done?
Fate was a malicious devil, but she would take the

reins of her own destiny in both hands and she would never give in.

The rest of the weekend passed without any opportunity for Con to fulfil his promise. Either that or he was playing a game of wait and see, drawing out her sense of the inevitable to its limits, so that when the time seemed right she would be so desperate for him he would be able to take her without any resistance.

If, early on the Saturday evening, she had believed she was simply a cog in the Arlington machine, that brief encounter in her room had thoroughly dispelled the idea, suggesting a dangerous alternative and setting other wheels in motion again. Yet throughout the rest of the weekend Con seemed determined to give her the kid-glove treatment while leaving her in no doubt about his desire for her. It was an odd experience, as if by holding off he was deliberately fanning her desire. Whenever they chanced to meet, the air crackled around them with the combustible energy of desire. Kim felt he was so confident of victory that he was simply sitting back as if to say, 'Look, I can outwait you because I know you're going to be mine.'

Safely back in London, Kim called in at Lizzie's flat on the Monday lunchtime and, flinging herself down in a chair, tried to explain how she felt. 'I thought he wanted a casual affair at first. Then when we arrived at Abbaye it seemed to be confirmed by the way he seemed to have slotted me neatly into his workforce. I'd provide the dalliance for after-work hours. But then later——' and she explained about their encounter in her room and the role Lizzie's white lace dress had played, 'He treated me like something he was saving up to enjoy to the full when the time was right! I'm absolutely nerve-racked, Lizzie. Whatever shall I do? I can't give in to a man like that, first because I don't go around having casual flings and secondly because of who he is. I feel like running away, but I can't do that because it would be letting Ian down and— oh, Lizzie, he is so gorgeous, damn him!'

'Who, Ian?'

'No, fool! Take this seriously! It's important. I feel utterly terrible. What can I do?'

'He's held off this weekend, you say?'

'Only just. The air was electric whenever we met.'

'Perhaps he simply respects you and wants to give you time to make up your mind.' Lizzie smiled. 'Why on earth not?'

'But you don't understand. He's not that type. He's a bandit when it comes to women—he takes what he wants and to hell with how anybody else feels about it.'

'How do you know?'

Kim goggled. 'What on earth do you mean, how do I know? I *know* the man, don't I? I know what he's like in court, for a start. I've suffered him in action.'

'But do you know what he's like out of court?'

'Of course I do! I've just spent a weekend with him! He's a power maniac—all those workers kowtowing to him on the estate. He's Mister Big and he glories in it. He couldn't run an enterprise like that if he were the type to let other people have their own way, could he?'

'Maybe that's not the only way of looking at it. If there's a lot of organising to do for his uncle he's got to be pretty firm—and it doesn't mean he's a bandit when it comes to emotions either,' argued Lizzie reasonably.

'Oh, sometimes you're so naïve, Liz!' Kim got up and paced about the room. 'If you met him you'd know exactly what I'm talking about.'

'Are you sure you're not looking for excuses?'

'Excuses? What do I need excuses for?'

Lizzie gave her a dry smile. 'Think about it.' She too got up. 'I have to go back to college now. Put the key through the letter-box when you leave—and Kim, if you want to talk ring me this evening, OK?'

When she had gone Kim stood by the window, frowning down at the grey street with its dusty, inner-city plane trees. Lizzie could be most infuriating sometimes. Think about it, indeed! What on earth was there to think about?

CHAPTER SEVEN

THROUGH the following days thoughts of Con Arlington intervened with annoying frequency. Kim was kept busy by discussions with Ian about the Abbaye-sur-Lac project, and when that was settled she had to keep up with the rest of the work coming in. One commission took her to a health club, another to a chain of hairdressers, both of them small compared to Con's assignment, but it was the sort of work that had been the bread and butter of the agency so far, so she couldn't shirk it.

On the third day back she was interrupted by a phone call. Laura handed the receiver to her with a secret smile so that even before she heard the rich voice honeying down the line she guessed who was on the other end.

'I've been in court solidly this week and haven't been able to get away as I'd intended,' he began. 'I had hoped to get off early tomorrow in order to come up and see you, but it looks as if that plan has to be shelved too.' Before Kim could interrupt he went on, 'How about if you came down here instead?'

'But——'

'It's only an hour's drive and if you like you can stay the night at the flat.'

113

'But why do we need to meet?' she countered. There was nothing that would get her to stay the night at Con Arlington's place, so she didn't even bother considering that part of the invitation.

'I'm sorry, I put that rather baldly.' He cursed himself for rushing things. 'But I'm due back in court in a minute. We do need to talk, Kim, so say you'll come.'

It was true, there were things to discuss. Now she had talked to Ian one or two ideas had coalesced and she would have liked Con's opinion at some point.

He went on to suggest this himself. 'I thought you might need a couple of days to let things take shape,' he said, 'but it's time we talked now.'

Actually there was no real hurry, as Con himself very well knew, and the injected urgency in his words sounded false even to himself. But he had to see her. The last two days had been hell. It was a novel experience to have a woman on his mind to this extent, and he didn't understand why he was being driven so. If he could only talk her into bed, perhaps the obsession would leave him.

Kim gave a despairing look towards Ian's closed door. There would be no help from that quarter. 'Very well,' she agreed. 'I can drive down late tomorrow afternoon.' She paused. 'But I won't stay the night, I have to be back in the studio at nine and I don't fancy a dawn drive.'

Con bit back the obvious quip about dawn drives and merely murmured his assent. 'Come to my chambers when you get into town. I'll be here.' He rang off.

Kim sat for a moment or two staring at her drawing-board without seeing it. Up until the very moment she had heard Con's voice she had believed her efforts to put him into perspective had paid off. But just one syllable of those sexy cut-glass accents shattered any such illusions. It took twenty minutes and a cup of strong black coffee to get her mind back on her work. Even then his voice was a lingering musical theme for the rest of the day.

That evening she rang Lizzie. 'I can't get him out of my mind,' she told her. 'I wonder if I'm ill or something.'

Lizzie laughed. 'Yes, it's called love-sickness.'

'Don't be ridiculous!' exclaimed Kim, annoyed, 'I can't *love* the man—I know what a gangster he is. If I were the vengeful type I'd be plotting some dire retribution even now, but luckily for him I'm not. No, love is definitely out of the question. My theory is that it's something to do with overwork. I'll really have to take things easier. Trouble is, I just don't know what to do. I simply can't stop thinking about him. I wonder if it'd be best to see more of him—or less?'

'What do you want to do?' asked Lizzie cautiously, not wishing to get her head bitten off again.

'I don't want to see him at all, ever,' said Kim hastily, then she checked herself; even she knew that wasn't quite true.

Lizzie detected the note of doubt in her voice at once. 'If he wanted to see you—you wouldn't say no?'

'Apparently not,' and she told Lizzie about their meeting the next day. She frowned then. 'I feel I ought to see him a lot—to get him out of my system. He still has a certain mystique, and it's that that's feeding my obsession. Once he's demystified I'll be all right.'

'You're sure about that, are you?' asked Lizzie drily.

'Of course. It's the obvious answer, isn't it?'

'I don't know about obvious, but if you're in need of an escape hatch tomorrow night you can always stay here.'

By the time she rang off Kim had persuaded herself that she was right. If she could see enough of Con Arlington to prove to herself conclusively that he was the nasty type she knew he was, it would effect a cure in no time at all. After all, no one in their right mind would fall for a known out-and-out brute, would they?

As soon as Con saw her standing in chambers, clutching a big black leather bag stuffed with rough notes and sketches, he came over, an air of caution on his face that struck Kim as being out of character. There was obviously something on his mind. He didn't touch her when he gained her side, but hovered as if her air of self-possession, together with that rare, fragile beauty, was too fine for immediate contact.

'I thought we might have a drink round the corner first,' he began after giving her a brief nod, still careful to keep his distance. 'Lord knows I can do with one, and I'm sure you can after braving the tail-end of the rush-hour. I've booked a table for eight, by the way.' To her surprise he added casually, 'What time were you thinking of setting off back?'

'About ten, I suppose.' She hadn't thought about it, all her energies being concentrated on simply getting away safely out of his clutches when their talk was ended. She was confused to have won that round without a fight. It was almost as if he wanted to get rid of her.

He opened the door abruptly without replying and led her down the stairs and out into the courtyard past the parked cars. 'Ten o'clock, yes,' he agreed once they were settled in the cocktail bar of the Golden Fleece. 'That should give us ample time to talk things over.'

Kim eyed him dubiously. Given his typical self-confidence, he presumably expected that she wouldn't want to drive back at all, let alone at such a ridiculously early hour. No doubt he would try to organise it so that she was the one to do the asking. The drink-drive laws would work in his favour. He would no doubt expect her to feel grateful to him for letting her stay the night. What followed then would be as inevitable as destiny. He would reveal himself as the swine he really was and her feelings would return to normal.

She was looking up at him, unconscious of the effect of those slanting green eyes veiled seductively beneath thick lashes, her sweet, elfin face perfect in its frame of wild, dark hair, her aloof manner making the prospect of possession even more tantalising because of the possibility of failure. *'La Belle Dame Sans Merci,'* he murmured ironically. Kim smiled faintly at the allusion. It was difficult to believe he had ever seen himself in the role of lovesick swain now or at any other time in his no doubt chequered past.

Over their before-dinner drink Kim was waiting to see what he would do next. That first cool welcome just now might have been because he was genuinely preoccupied by his battle in court that day. It must take time to unwind even for someone who relished his job as much as Con obviously did.

But after a rather stilted conversation about summer holidays—for which neither of them had made any plans—they found themselves down to talking about the weather, Con with that same distant air as if he was mentally counting the minutes he had to endure her company, and Kim with a nerviness that was unlike her as she watched for any sign that he was suddenly going to change gear and pounce.

They were both so on edge they turned up at the Chelsea restaurant far too early. Con was like a cat on hot bricks.

Kim could see he was on edge, and judging by the way he had kept on looking at the clock above her head in the pub she wondered if he had a date with someone else later on. That would account for his eagerness to get to the restaurant. Perhaps he thought they could get their talk over even sooner than anticipated. She imagined some woman waiting for him back at his flat...her eyes closed and she shook her head slightly to rid it of an unexpectedly disturbing image of Con and this other faceless competitor. Competitor? She frowned again. She had opted out of this particular event as soon as she had learned his name. Heavens, he was the enemy! There was no way she could forget that.

'All right?' he asked, leaning forward slightly. The waiter had lit a candle and it guttered between them like something alive that had been trapped.

'Fine.' Kim looked away.

'I thought you frowned.'

'Did I?' Her glance fluttered towards his, then fell in confusion. His eyes were unfathomable—such bright blue, they took in everything but gave nothing away. It was unfair. 'I have a slight headache,' she fibbed. 'It's nothing.'

'Been busy?'

'Yes.'

'As usual, I suppose?'

'Yes.'

This is brilliant, she thought. Conversationalist of the year. What on earth can I say to him when he looks at me like that?

She stared miserably at her plate. Of course she didn't really want to get any closer to him, but she had decided that to do so would cure her obsession. Now it looked as if she wasn't going to get the chance with this show of scintillating repartee. Boredom would drive him away before the pudding. She would have to try harder, for she simply couldn't let him get away before she had a chance to get him out of her system by planned overdose. For if she failed, then what? Would she be doomed to obsession for the rest of her life? She pulled herself together and tried to find a few faults. There were none. Apart from the obvious, that one real fault that made the relationship impossible.

'How's the case going this week?' she asked, trying to sound bright and interested. 'Or aren't you supposed to talk about things like that to outsiders?'

'It's been front-paging in the gutter Press since Monday—though I suppose you only read the quality dailies?'

'Actually I haven't had time to see the papers at all this week,' she confessed, feeling ignorant and stupid. What case was he talking about? She didn't know.

'Been too busy?' Con replied generously.

Back to square one, she thought. End of conversation. 'What was it you wanted to talk about?' she asked in desperation as the meal dragged on.

Maybe if she could get him talking her own woeful ignorance wouldn't be so obvious.

'I wanted to know how your ideas were taking shape,' he replied at once.

Kim took the brevity of his reply for a lack of interest. If he's as bored as he looks then damn him, she thought. I'm not going to put myself out to explain what Ian and I have cooked up if he's already losing interest. He can wait until we send in our report like all our other clients.

'Let's say we've had one or two ideas,' she admitted after a long pause.

Con was sitting just staring at her with a far-away expression on his face, obviously thinking about something entirely different, and didn't even reply.

'It's such a picturesque place at this time of year,' she ploughed on, struggling to find something to say about Abbaye-sur-Lac, 'with everything coming into bloom,' she added lamely.

His eyes were an indescribable colour, light, liquid, like Venetian glass—no, more expressive than glass—like blue flame. She could have talked about *them* for hours, if asked. 'It'll be almost impossible to do a bad job on the place,' she said, searching for anything that would grip his attention again. 'When it's tarted up it might lose some of its charm, though.' She knew she was babbling, but how could she think straight when he looked at her like that? Surely he could see right inside her?

Now he merely nodded. Kim looked glumly down at her plate again. She would go round to Lizzie's after this. Maybe there would even be time to go out for a quick drink in the new wine bar she had mentioned. Con Arlington wasn't the only one with a social life that was more gripping than the job that had brought them together. She watched him glare round the restaurant at the other diners, obviously searching for their waiter.

He's desperate to get away, she registered glumly. What made me think he might be interested? Obviously he kisses every woman, just to see how amenable we are. If we're not, well, I suppose he's got so many lined up it doesn't matter a damn if one or two are unwilling.

'Let's not bother with coffee.' Con was already beckoning the waiter for the bill, and Kim bent to pick up her bag so that he couldn't see the expression on her face. She could be back at home before eleven. She didn't feel like the wine bar after all. An earlyish sort of night might do her good.

In a minute they were outside. This is where he says goodnight, thought Kim.

'It's a great evening,' he announced, exaggerating wildly, she thought. Cloud lay in banks above the city roofs and looked as heavy as her heart. 'Want to go for a short stroll by the river before you go back?' He stepped away, half turning to invite her to follow.

'River?' Kim spoke as if she hadn't realised the Thames flowed through London. She followed him

to the corner of the street. At the kerb he paused
and took her arm.

'Don't cross yet, the lights haven't changed,' he
warned, holding on to her.

Why the river? she wondered. She let him lead
her across the road to the other side, expecting him
to release her arm as soon as they got there, but he
kept it, hooked in a brotherly sort of fashion
through his own. She felt her legs begin to turn to
jelly again and stumbled. Con used it as an excuse
to put his arm about her waist.

They walked along the Embankment in silence.
The sun streaked the sky dramatically behind the
black fingers of the power station on the other side
of a river turned molten by the westering sun. Kim
felt as if she were walking inside a dream. Any
moment now she would wake up to find herself
driving back alone through the suburbs.

'Kim?' Con turned to her when they reached the
Albert Bridge with its necklace of lights and looked
down at her with a look of indecision on his face.
Then before she could stop him he was pulling her
roughly into his arms. His head came down and he
was enveloping her in a kiss that shut out the roar
of passing traffic and the inquisitive glances of
passers-by, and it seemed for a moment as if they
were locked in an island of light all their own.

Kim's mind was bereft of all desire to resist. Once
he's de-romanticised, she told herself wildly, I'll be
able to see him for the swine he really is. Stripped

of all romantic illusion, I'll be able to forget him for good.

Next she knew he would ask her to go back to his flat, and once there he would immediately show himself up as the slick, faithless womaniser she guessed he was. All she had to do was sit back and wait for him to confirm it. Then she would escape to Lizzie's flat for the night, heart and soul intact once more. End of story.

They both stepped back at the same moment. 'Let's go,' Con suggested.

Half closing her eyes, Kim gave a small nod, wondering how far away his flat was. 'Yes, yes, Con, let's go.'

He kissed her again as they stood on a traffic island in the King's Road. It was after he had told her they might as well walk the long way back to the car. By making a detour they passed within a few hundred yards of his flat, and he pointed it out to her as if he had no intention of trying to talk her into going back there with him.

Kim took it as an invitation, however, turning sharply in that direction so that their two bodies collided unexpectedly. Con looked surprised, then gripped her tightly as if to prevent her from stumbling.

'I suppose you could call in for a minute and look over the original plans for Abbaye,' he suggested dubiously.

Kim registered the expression on his face. That split second's look of doubt set off all kinds of suspicions. 'What a good idea. I'd love to,' she replied swiftly, to his evident astonishment. Trying to look as nonchalant as she could, she was horribly aware of her heart climbing rapidly into her mouth. What if there was no one else there after all and he turned back into his guise of arch-seducer? It was all very well calling his bluff now that he looked tame and seemed genuinely not to want her to come back with him, but that might only be because he was afraid of what, or who, she would discover at the flat to spoil his future plans.

When they at last came up to the smart black door with its heavy wrought-brass fittings and its perfect wistaria curling over the porch she had a moment's panic. Then she thought she saw his hands shake as he put the key in the lock, though it might have been a transference of her own feelings, because he turned to her on the threshold with a lift of his eyebrows and asked coolly enough, 'Nervous?'

Before she could deny it he went on, 'You don't have to be. I promise to behave.'

'I suppose you say that to everyone,' she joked shakily.

'True,' he agreed with a nervous laugh, 'but this time I really mean it.' He looked as if he wanted to say something else, but obviously had second thoughts, merely pushing her on ahead of him without another word.

She stepped through into the entrance hall. A stained-glass window high up and the pale champagne colours of the décor gave the place a pleasing tranquillity. But there was a feeling of sheer dread in the pit of her stomach. Had she bitten off more than she could chew? Con was an experienced seducer, she could already tell that, and she was comparatively innocent. What if things got out of hand? She was playing with fire, fully aware of how difficult he was to resist and how quickly their mutual attraction seemed to flare up with the speed of a fire-storm.

Yet she had to find out what he was really like. She had to have her prejudices confirmed. Only then would she have the ammunition to fight this obsessive emotion that appeared to have swamped her mind and overtaken her reason.

Her strongest protection would be her memory of the past. She would cling to that, to the memory of the grief this man had caused. Ahead lay a test of her own loyalty to her mother—and it would be a test of Con Arlington too.

He didn't embrace her as soon as they got inside as she hoped and feared. Instead he went around switching all the lights full on. Then he went over to the stereo and put on a tape. Kim expected it to be something smoochy as befitted the occasion, but it was a Blues Brothers number that would normally have made her feel like getting up and dancing. Before she could say anything Con disappeared into the adjoining kitchen and she heard him crashing about with cups and saucers.

'Can I help?' She stood in the doorway, emotions warring at the sight of him making such an inexplicable hash of things. Coffee beans had somehow shot out of the jar he was holding and spilled all over the floor.

He kicked at them as if not quite sure how to get rid of them.

'Is there a brush and pan?' she asked, not intending to do the job but hoping to offer a helpful hint.

'I don't know.' He looked around helplessly, then seemed to make a big effort. 'In here, I think.' He had to reach out to open the cupboard she was by now leaning against. The slight brush of her skirt against the back of his hand made him jerk back as if he expected to be accused of assault.

Somehow the beans were disposed of, but by then he remembered the bottle of wine he had decorked. Ready for the planned seduction scene, she registered.

'It seems stupid to let it go to waste,' he explained, reading the label as if he had forgotten what was in it.

Kim had expected wine. For, of course, he would have to get her a little tipsy. But she wasn't stupid. She would sip it, pretending to drink more than she did. As soon as he imagined she was helpless with drink he would be more likely to show his true colours than if he thought she was stone-cold sober. How she would dispose of the wine she wasn't drinking she didn't bother to plan. Time enough for niceties later.

He brought in the bottle, together with two crystal glasses, and poured for two. The bottle seemed to empty alarmingly. Perhaps the glasses were larger than they looked. Kim glanced around for a convenient plant and was relieved to find that there was one if she needed it. Con sat down on the far side of a fragile-looking glass coffee-table as soon as he saw her ensconced in the middle of his vast sofa. Silence fell.

'I'll get those plans out in a minute.'

'Good.' She was amazed to find she had drained her glass already. Was she over the limit now? she wondered, as he refilled it. If so she would have to get a taxi to Lizzie's.

They played cat and mouse till the tape ran out. Conversation was easier than it had been in the restaurant. The kiss, though unmentioned, seemed to have eased the tension. Another bottle of wine appeared, and disappeared before Kim realised with a jolt that it was half past twelve. Time seemed to have flown. She took a deep breath, then ploughed on with the fatal words, 'I suppose I ought to be driving back.'

'Nonsense,' Con replied swiftly as she had known he would. 'You'll be flagged down and lose your licence.' He seemed desperate for her to stay. 'There's a spare bed—use that. I can't allow you to drive.'

He must imagine things are going perfectly according to plan, she thought with an ironic nod towards the part she herself was playing in the charade. He no doubt imagined she was walking innocently into his carefully laid trap. True, until now, he had behaved impeccably, just as he had promised, and she had to force herself to believe he wasn't as harmless as he seemed right now. In a minute or two he would reveal his true colours at last. After a little more talk of this and that, he showed her the bathroom and the spare room and apologised for not having any female attire she could wear in bed. Still scoring points heavily for the perfect behaviour, he stood at a respectable distance and wished her goodnight. Then shortly, to her intense surprise, she found herself alone.

Kim gaped at the door that had closed so decidedly between them. Her thoughts in turmoil, she quickly undressed and began to comb her hair. All the time her ears were pricked for the sound of returning footsteps. But the flat was silent.

What was she to make of him? she asked herself. Was he a gentleman after all? Had she got him quite wrong? Surely not! But what if Lizzie was right and she had misunderstood him from the first and he did in fact have a genuine respect for her? But that couldn't be so, could it? She was confused. Respect? From a man like Con Arlington? More likely he was merely indifferent. But how could she tell? She had nothing and no one to compare him with.

She peered at herself in the bedroom mirror before sliding between the sheets. She looked much as usual. No sudden disfigurement had appeared by magic to put him off. There was no unsightly spinach stuck between her teeth. Her mascara hadn't given her two panda eyes. Of course, her hair was nearly black. In the half-light from the bedside lamp it glimmered like silk, and she knew Con was a man with a penchant for redheads. But could any man be so single-minded? She knew she herself would feel turned on by Con Arlington if he had blond, red, green or no hair at all.

With a feeling like lead she drew up the duvet. If there was a knock on her door in the early hours she would of course repulse any advances. But at least she would feel justified in thinking ill of him all those years when he was just a name, and, paradoxically, her spirits would have risen a little to know she was desired by him now. But it seemed despite the magical kisses they shared she was either not his type—or he was everything he claimed to be and he had passed the test with flying colours. The knowledge brought her no satisfaction whatever.

But she needn't have worried. Next morning everything was turned upside down with a vengeance.

CHAPTER EIGHT

REMEMBERING that Kim had to set off early in order to get to the studio by nine o'clock, Con woke her at seven, breakfast already sizzling away nicely, with no sign of last night's ineptness in the kitchen. He was cool, amusing, talked neither too much nor too little, and Kim, thoroughly confused, had decided silently over the coffee to give him the benefit of the doubt. He was that rare phenomenon, a true gentleman. His wild words at Abbaye had meant nothing at all.

She helped him wash up, then went into the hall to get her things, talking to him over her shoulder as she did so. A sound at the front door showed that the postman had stuffed a pile of letters through the letterbox. Without thinking she went to pick them up, intending to go back into the kitchen with them.

Then she stopped. A large picture postcard was lying on top of the pile on the mat, and somehow her eyes had slid over the bold childish handwriting before she could stop them.

'Can't wait to be in your bed at the weekend, darling! (Hope the postman doesn't blush!) Love and kisses, Ginny.'

Kim's blood froze.

Con's impeccable behaviour, then, had a reason. Here it was, stark and clear. It wasn't that she didn't interest him, but that somebody else interested him more.

So much for her plan to discover the real Con Arlington. There had been no deception at all. He was as he had told her—a man with a roving eye, yes, but a man for whom fidelity was no problem either. She heard him coming out of the kitchen and she slid the card in with the others before turning and handing the whole lot over to him. She was ashamed to have read it at all, but the words had hit her before she could stop them.

'I'll go now,' she said, wondering why her voice didn't waver.

'I'll just get my keys.'

'No, I'll go by tube. You don't need to be in your office as early as this.'

'Don't be silly. I'm not letting you go by public transport. You'll probably have hours to wait.'

'Please, I'd rather,' she protested.

'I insist.'

Looking at his face, Kim gave in. What difference did it make? Another quarter of an hour by his side and then she would be free of him. Till next time. And the time after that. And forever in her heart.

She moved stiffly on ahead. Now she knew with hideous clarity that Lizzie had been right. She should have done as she advised; she should have thought about it. If she had been able to admit to her true feelings right from the start, she wouldn't have laid herself open to this blinding, searing white heat of pain that throbbed through her. Con was innocent. It wasn't his fault he had made her feel this way; it was her own fault for loving him. And she did love him—madly, desperately. It had taken something as trivial as a postcard from another girl to make her see the truth. She must have loved him from that very first meeting. It was only the confusion of discovering who he was that had clouded the issue.

Con watched her get into her Triumph Stag. He bent his head as if about to cover her pale, enigmatic face with kisses, then rejected the idea as if he thought such a show of feeling would embarrass her. She was cool, self-possessed.

Yet she watched him in her driving-mirror as she drove away until he was a tiny figure standing by the kerb.

'So he approves of all our ideas, does he?' Ian looked impatient. Kim was being very unforthcoming this morning.

'To be honest,' she admitted after another long pause, 'he didn't seem to care a damn. Don't ask me why he wanted me to go up to town. We scarcely mentioned the project at all.'

'Then what the devil did you talk about all evening?'

'Nothing much,' she replied truthfully. 'I think he was probably preoccupied with this case he's fighting.'

'Yes, it's making quite a splash.'

'Is it?' Kim looked blank.

'Anyway,' said Ian briskly, 'you're off back to Montpellier this weekend, so when you get started he'll probably show a bit more interest. Make sure you liaise with him at every stage. I don't want to waste time and money on anything he doesn't really want.'

'I don't think he'll be in Montpellier this weekend,' she told him. In her misery she hadn't thought to mention it before they parted, and Con hadn't mentioned it either.

Ian looked perplexed. 'Funny, I thought he said he was.' Still chuntering, he wandered into his next-door office.

'Kim?'

She recognised the voice instantly. It was nearly lunchtime. Laura had already started worrying about booking a standby and whether it would be for one or two. Ian said one thing, Kim another. But now Con himself came straight to the point.

'I'm really tied up here with this case. It's one of those stubborn ones that drag on and on.'

'So you won't be coming to Montpellier this weekend?' she asked helpfully. Better to get it over with. He was a free agent, and he had behaved like a gentleman. What more did she want? Even so, she tensed for his reply.

When it came she gaped at the receiver in astonishment. 'Not come?' he exclaimed. 'Of course I'm coming. Why ever did you think I wasn't?' He gave a warm chuckle. 'I'm looking forward to it. At least this weekend I won't have to go round checking the building regulations and generally playing Commissar for Uncle. I'll be your lackey instead. I'm afraid it can't have been much fun for you last time, tagging around with an army of builders.'

'Oh,' she said. There didn't seem anything else to say.

'I've managed to fix a ride in a private aircraft leaving from that airfield near you. That's why I didn't mention it last night—I wasn't sure whether I could fix it up. I thought it would save you the drive back into town. I'll get away from here as soon as I can.'

He rang off. Kim felt numb. What had happened to Ginny? Some last-minute hitch? Con didn't sound like a man disappointed. Just the opposite— he sounded as if he was positively looking forward to spending a weekend with her. She bent her head to her work. There was no way of making it make sense. She would just have to wait and see.

A dozen red roses arrived for Kim at lunchtime. After her initial surprise she viewed them with suspicion. What game was he playing? Thwarted by this Ginny, had he immediately turned his attentions to her? He certainly lost no time.

She let him into the front sitting-room of her small cottage a quarter of a mile away from the studio at half past four that afternoon, noticing that he saw the roses straight away where they were crammed into a plain white vase on the windowsill. She didn't mention them and neither did he.

He looked round the tiny place and gave her a puzzled frown. 'Are you just moving out, or just moving in?'

'I've been renting this place for two years—but I'm still not sure it's permanent,' she told him, lifting her chin. 'I was offered a job with Ian as soon as I left art college. It was meant to be a stopgap until I could decide what I really wanted to do. Somehow the business took off and we started to build up a profitable list of clients between us, so I just sort of stayed. I bought myself a decent car instead of a house. That way I don't have any excuse to stay if I change my mind.'

'You don't strike me as the indecisive type.'

'I'm not—usually.'

'So?'

Kim felt like telling him to mind his own business, but merely shrugged.

But Con wouldn't let it go. 'Hoping to move out to get married, perhaps?' He moved closer, staring down at her with that searching blue-eyed look of his.

'Go to hell!' she muttered, moving away. 'Have you no imagination?'

To Kim it seemed as if his expression of blank incomprehension was pure front. 'My real home was handed over to that man and his girlfriend, remember? I simply don't feel like putting down roots again!' she exclaimed. 'Don't pretend you don't understand.' She gave him a glare and walked through into the kitchen. Her bag was already packed for the weekend and there was nothing to stop them leaving right now, but there was something more important keeping her here. Con followed her.

'You could afford somewhere permanent if you wanted to, couldn't you?' he quizzed, trapping her between the sink and the corner cupboard.

'Mind your own damned business!'

'It is my business!'

'Nothing I do is your business—apart from the job you're paying me for.'

'Your lips are my business,' he said huskily, bringing his own close to her throat so that she could feel the warmth of his body reaching out to her as they hovered over her skin.

She pushed him hard in the chest, but he didn't yield. 'You've kissed me several times,' she said hoarsely. 'Always against my will.'

His derisive laugh cut in. 'Against your will? Really?'

'Your pride won't let you admit it,' she went on. 'It just happens that you're not everyone's type and for once you're going to have to accept defeat.' She caught sight of the roses through the doorway. 'You imagine a corny gesture like a bunch of flowers is going to have me dropping at your feet, don't you? Well, I'm sorry,' she drew herself up, 'it doesn't work.'

'I think I'll kiss you again,' he murmured, ignoring her words, 'against your will, as usual.' There was a dangerous look in his eyes, his confidence obvious that once he held her her will would turn to jelly as before. Sure that if she failed to keep him at arm's length this time everything would be lost and he would be able to take her up and use her and discard her to suit himself, as perhaps he had done with the mysterious Ginny this weekend, she gave him another hard push, her hands slipping ineffectually against the hard muscles of his chest as he put both arms right round her and pulled her towards him.

'Don't I deserve a little reward for behaving so beautifully last night?' he murmured against her hair.

'Most men would regard behaviour like that as natural,' she retorted weakly.

His mouth rested against her hairline. She could feel its soft pressure on her skin.

'Don't, Con! I'll hate you forever if you do!' She tried to twist away, moving her head from side to side.

'I thought you said you already did hate me,' he replied, bringing his head down again when she stopped struggling.

'I can't hate like that—it seems—it seems pointless somehow.'

'So don't hate me now.'

'I do! I do!'

'No, Kimmy, don't hate me.'

'But I can't forget. I can't forgive. And I know I would be stupid to trust——' She broke off, already afraid she had given too much away.

'I'm quite harmless, darling!' Con's eyes were brilliant, cloudless skies promising unlimited happiness. She knew it was only an illusion. Like sunshine before rain.

Tears of frustration welled in her eyes. She wanted to be very, very angry, but there was no way of expressing it when he held her like this. Her body yearned to give in and she had to fight against herself as well as against the power of his formidable purpose. 'Why me?' she demanded, her voice made high with emotion.

'Because you're the most beautiful creature I've ever held in my arms.'

'Easy to say,' she countered. 'And of course you always have the right words on the tip of your tongue.' Somehow his grip had slackened as if he realised it was going to be a fight, and he had already told her he didn't want that. She slipped easily out of his arms, going to stand in the doorway leading back into the sitting-room. Once at a safe distance she found it easier to think.

'I don't care how much you're paying Image Design for this job, if you do this again I shall throw it in. If necessary I shall resign from the firm. There's nothing keeping me here. I can easily get another job. And as you can see, half my things are already packed.'

For a moment there was a stunned silence. Con's face gave nothing away at all and she thought he was going to start arguing with her, but his blue eyes only narrowed slightly as he said, 'That's laying it on the line fair and square. So what are we waiting for? Let's go.'

'But do you agree? No more?' She spread her hands, feeling melodramatic to be making such a fuss about a mere kiss. Except that, to her, it wasn't a mere kiss at all, but a key to heaven and hell.

'No more kisses? No more touching? No more red roses? What sort of life do you want, Kim?' His voice had roughened and he covered the distance between them in a couple of strides, taking her savagely into his arms, all humour having fled. His eyes swept her face with the touch of ice. 'Are you trying to drive me out of my mind? Can't you see how I feel about you? I know you feel something—I've seen your face when I kiss you. You want me, Kim, don't deny it. You're as crazy for me as I am for you!'

Flames of desire seemed to leap between them. Kim felt as if she were standing on the edge of a fiery abyss. Somehow she managed to speak. 'I don't want you,' she croaked. 'You're the man who killed my mother!' The words were out before she could stop them.

For a moment Con's face simply registered shock. Then he gave her a look of pure disbelief. 'Wait a minute, you can't——' He tried to take her in his arms again, but she moved out of reach.

'Keep away from me!' She was trembling from head to foot to think how close to going over to the enemy she had been. What would her mother have thought if she had known how close to surrendering to her 'young Daniel' she had been?

The clock, her mother's carriage clock, chimed the half-hour.

'Hell, we're late.' Con looked undecided. Then he moved towards the door. 'Tell me about all this later.' Ignoring her request not to touch her, he gripped her strongly by the upper arm and with an odd expression on his face hustled her towards the door. 'Key? Passport?'

'Yes.' She pulled her arm away and when they were outside locked the door, then followed him to the car.

Silent on the short drive to the airfield, and relieved to discover that the presence of another two passengers in the small cabin made intimate conversation impossible, Kim was also relieved to find that even when they reached Abbaye-sur-Lac the place was swarming with visitors and that, late, with only enough time to rush up to change for dinner, there was still no time for the promised talk. She dreaded the interrogation that would have to follow her accusation, and the thought of opening up all that old pain was abhorrent.

Con would never understand. And she felt half convinced that, once he got her to talk, he would be able to make mincemeat of anything she said. It would only be the strength of her resistance that would be a palisade against his attack, and, beleaguered, knowing that it would take so little to make her hand herself over to him, body and soul, she was determined not to give an inch.

She dressed carefully. Con had warned her it might be a dressy affair. 'It's the old devil's birthday tomorrow, and tradition has it we assemble the evening before.'

'I wish I'd known. I haven't brought him anything.'

'He'd be distressed to know you minded.'

He left her then. Since her outburst at the cottage he had worn an odd expression on his face, and she felt it wasn't simply that he hadn't had the opportunity to delve into what she had said then. There was something more. It made her wonder.

Her uneasiness was confirmed when this time he knocked on her door to take her down. His eyes flickered blankly over her, saying nothing about the dress she wore, his lips, when he brought himself to speak, scarcely moving. 'We're late.' He stepped to one side, his eyes avoiding hers, and she stepped on ahead down the corridor.

A subdued noise came from outside in the direction of the terrace, and she took his arm when they reached the bottom of the stairs, feeling suddenly in need of protection, but from what she couldn't tell.

Later she understood. It had been a premonition. Con left her as soon as he had given her a drink and disappeared into the thick of the partying guests. Obviously he had family duties to perform, old friends to greet, new friends, she observed, overhearing the introductions, he had to make. But equally obviously he wanted nothing more than to cut her out of his life. Yet what she had said was true. If he couldn't face the truth then that was his problem.

Thoughts like this made her feel utterly wretched, but what else could she think? With no opportunity to have a proper talk the thoughts just churned around inside her head.

She hung about on the fringes by herself until Mariette spied her and introduced her to one or two unattached men, but her French wasn't good enough to cope with the witty repartee that seemed to be the order of the day, and after stonewalling the chatting-up process as politely as she could, Kim managed to drift away to a corner of the stone balustrade separating the terrace from the lawns below.

One or two couples were walking between the flower beds, perambulating in and out of the rose-laced arbours. She could see the glow of cigarettes in the dark, hear the intimate murmur of voices, an occasional peal of distant laughter. Music drifted from out of the house; a sickle moon rode high in a purple night sky. Her whole being was filled with a longing she couldn't explain. It made her feel empty, with a desolation unknown to her since childhood when the endless arguments between her parents had driven her to the solitude of her own room.

She turned to look back at the house. Every light was on. Con's uncle, in whose honour all these people were gathered together, had appeared on the balcony above the terrace. He was surrounded by a bevy of young women. She heard the clink of glasses, the pop of champagne corks. Couples began to dance, at the old man's request. No one in all the crowd seemed as miserable and confused as she was.

Then she felt a hand round her waist, pulling her off the parapet, and she bumped against the soft, over-fed body of a stranger. It was one of the men Mariette had introduced to her—willing to try again.

'*Dansez avec moi?*' he murmured in her ear, sliding his hands along the slender body.

'*Non, s'il vous plaît.*' She tried to step out of the man's embrace, but he had arms like an octopus. Over his head she saw a face peering down at her. It appeared and disappeared through the bobbing heads. It was Con. He was dancing with Lisette, the redhead nestling against the white shoulder of his dinner jacket, her arms twined possessively around his neck.

Reluctantly Kim took to the floor. Her partner was shorter than she was and seemed to imagine that an invitation to dance was a prelude to all kinds of physical liberties. She stepped back suddenly to avoid the undulations of his embrace and a voice in English cut in, saying, 'You're wasting your time, Claude. This is the original English ice-maiden.'

She turned blazing eyes on the speaker, but Con, somehow depositing Lisette into the surprised Claude's arms, swept her into his own and led her swiftly down the terrace steps to the garden.

'What do you think you're doing?' The words rasped in her ear.

'What does it look like?'

'It looks as if you're going to finish up in a situation you can't handle,' he snarled. 'Again.'

'And you look like being your usual high-handed self,' retorted Kim, digging in her heels as he tried to lead her out of sight of the house.

Instead of pulling her after him he turned, folding her into his arms, and while she felt her limbs weaken in confusion at the sudden touch of his hard body against hers, he took advantage of the moment to propel her towards an arbour of clipped yew. By the time she was able to struggle against him he was holding her tightly in his arms in its shadowy seclusion.

'I've been looking forward to this thrash all week as I sweated it out in court,' he told her roughly. 'I fondly imagined we might be able to enjoy ourselves, forget our differences, even.' He paused. 'What I hadn't counted on was seeing you in the arms of a sweaty little man twice your age and,' he paused again, his face becoming grimmer, 'and finding myself accused of murder.'

'Let me go, Con Arlington! I've nothing to say.'

'You want a bet?' he replied belligerently, tilting her chin. 'Let me see your face.' He pulled her roughly back as she tried to get away. 'Look at me, damn you! No, stop struggling,' he rasped when she fought back. He held her in such a way she had no choice but to look up into his eyes. 'That's better,' he said, almost forgetting what he had been going to say. 'Now tell me again what you said at the cottage.'

'It's nothing. Let me go!'

'If it's nothing why are you looking at me like that?'

'Like what?' She tried to brazen it out, hiding her misery of a few minutes ago with a hardness to match his own. But it failed miserably. He was having none of it.

'Kim, I can stand here all night if need be. You should know by now that I never let go until I've got the truth. The gutter Press have got me right on that at least. Now come on, what did you mean? Tell!'

CHAPTER NINE

'CAN WE sit down or something? I can't talk while you're holding me like this.'

Suspicious that it was some sort of escape attempt, Con allowed her to sit on the wooden seat inside the arbour, himself standing in the entrance as if to prevent her from making a dash for it.

'You know what happened five years ago to East Leigh,' Kim began miserably. 'How do you imagine Mother took it?'

'What did she expect?'

'Not that, for sure,' replied Kim bitterly.

'But she didn't expect to swan back from Mexico and walk straight into a property like that, did she? Who do you think took on the upkeep all those years she was away?'

'Yes, but he did that for one very good reason— so that he and his mistress could get their nasty thieving hands on it when the time was right!'

'Your father took it on when it was in need of repair. He spent thousands on the place.'

'And what is it worth now? Tens of thousands?'

'Quite a lot,' Con smiled faintly. 'But he wanted to provide a home for you—that's what the tug-of-love case was all about, wasn't it?'

'How would you know? You must have been still at school when all that was going on!'

'True.' He paused. 'I was probably a grubby fourth-former.' He laughed, then seeing her serious face added, 'It still doesn't alter the fact that he wanted it for you.'

'Let me correct you, Mr Arlington, he wanted *me* because he wanted East Leigh.'

Con's expression told her what he thought of this.

'It's true!' she exploded. 'I should know. He'd worked out that the property would cost him nothing but a few repairs. All he had to do was sit back and watch it appreciate.'

'That's true.' Con looked thoughtful. 'He's a businessman. He obviously knew what he was doing.'

'Thank you. That's exactly what I'm trying to say.'

He came to sit beside her. 'I don't know all the ins and outs of your family's affairs, but it seemed clear-cut at the time. East Leigh belonged to your maternal grandfather. Instead of leaving it to any of his children, he left it to you, to be held in trust until your twenty-first birthday. Your mother was living in it then and presumably he imagined you would both live there together.'

'But he died before the divorce, never realising that his son-in-law, my father, would fight for custody of me and then push Mother out.'

'I don't know about pushing her out. Didn't she go gallivanting off to Mexico with some musician or other?'

'You make it sound sleazy and immoral!'

'Wasn't it?'

'Not unless you have a very warped, Victorian attitude to life.'

'Perhaps I have.'

Kim gave him a look of utter derision.

'She left you behind,' he pointed out.

'I was handed over by the courts to my father when I was ten, remember? After Mother's reputation had been thoroughly blackened, of course. No wonder she looked for solace elsewhere! She wasn't even allowed to visit me. It left nothing for her in England.'

'I—oh, was that it?'

'You should know. Your beloved uncle was acting for my father, I believe. Surely he kept you informed when you took over?'

'I was only about eighteen or nineteen myself and was determined to do anything but go into the law as the family dictated, so I deliberately never got involved before it was clear there was no choice.' Con gave her a narrowed look. 'Are you trying to tell me there was a miscarriage of justice?'

'I'm not trying to say anything,' she replied bitterly, recalling his words when he forced her to take on the job at Abbaye-sur-Lac. 'I'm saying that you got it wrong. You and your clan, you Arlingtons.'

'No, the law side of the family are the Forbes. Nothing to do with the Arlingtons,' he corrected.

'Does it matter?'

'It makes a difference.'

'Oh?' She didn't know what he was getting at, but she couldn't bear to listen to him any longer. She rose to her feet. It couldn't matter now what he said. The damage had been done long ago.

'Don't go,' he said urgently.

'Why ever not? We've nothing more to say to each other.'

'What happened, Kim? What happened to your mother?' He reached out to drag her back.

'No!' She shook her head, snatching her arms away. Suddenly it was all too much. Here she was, consorting with the enemy, listening to his lies, to the subterfuge, to Con Arlington pretending he didn't know what had led up to her mother's flight from England—the reason for her subsequent return, and all the horror of what followed. He must have known. And what was worse, he didn't care. One look at those enigmatic blue eyes showed that. All he wanted now was to lull her into acceptance so that she could take the place of Ginny, or Lisette, or one of the others he had presumably tired of. Well, it wasn't going to happen.

She began to walk rapidly from out of the arbour, ignoring his call to return and talk things out. When he caught up with her, she spun round angrily, saying. 'You expect to be able to talk your way out of it and I'm sure you can, given the chance. But you're not going to get the chance. It's your job to talk your way out of things, and we all know you're so very good at your job, Mr Arlington. But sometimes the talking has to stop and the facts have to speak for themselves. In real life——' But she didn't get a chance to go on, for he spun her back into his arms with a hissed exclamation.

'All right, I agree,' he announced, 'the talking has to stop. Let's allow the facts to speak, Kim. Fact, I feel crazy for you when you're in my arms. Fact, you feel the same way about me—no, don't deny it, I can read it in your eyes. You try to pretend you feel nothing, and half the time you take me in, but now, look.' He ran a finger sensually down the side of her cheek, not stopping at the jaw but letting it trickle slowly lower, down the soft skin of her long neck, circling and sliding to the soft mound at the top of her dress. The shudder this provoked was not lost on him, and his lips tightened in a smile of triumph. 'Fact, darling, you want me. Fact, I want you. Fact, as I told you before, we're going to dine like royalty, and I don't mean at table with a lot of guests—I mean alone, naked, in bed.'

Through the tracery of wild roses that shrouded the wall she could see the moon and the light of one bright star. The air was flower-scented, heady with summer warmth. Con pressed her trembling body against his own, caressing her completely from the nape of her neck to the firm thighs in their thin silk. She was surprised to feel him trembling and for an age he simply held her against his own body as if waiting for some kind of sign that she had given in, but when she tried to bring a protest to her lips it came out like a feeble croak, midway between assent and denial.

He smoothed the tangle of dark hair from her brow and kissed her forehead, then he lifted the hair at her nape, pressing kisses deeply into the hairline, kneading his cheek against the side of her head, holding off the moment when she knew their lips would have to meet.

Her head tilted and when she opened her eyes she was looking at the moon. 'It's not fair, Con,' she groaned. 'I really don't want—I can't——'

His voice was rough with feeling. 'Darling, what do you think I'm going to do? Take you against your will? When we make love for the first time it's not going to be like this. You're going to come to me willingly, joyfully, because you want me. Do you think I would settle for anything less? Is that what you think of me?' He lifted his head and his eyes were only a few inches from her own, and they were full of an uncharacteristic indecision. He went on. 'The trouble is when I hold you like this I think it might be best for us both if I ignored your protests, took you, slaked my need, gave you what you're dying for. But then what? Where would we go from there, with all our bridges burnt? What then?'

'Please——' she breathed, unsure whether she was pleading for or against his proposal. Her body gave its own answer. They both swayed, a knife-edge of desire waiting to topple them into ecstasy.

'If you were anyone else nothing would be easier. I would take you, love you, and when the time came we would part as friends,' he murmured hoarsely against the side of her neck. 'But with you it's different. I don't want a quick affair. I want...' He stopped speaking and it seemed as if he was afraid to confess what was closest to his heart.

Music still floated across the garden and a group of party guests came down the terrace steps, laughing as they moved into the darkness. Further away, night shadows offered deeper concealment. Kim yearned and feared it, drawn to it as Con began to turn her away from the house, yet trembling to take the first step that would signal her surrender.

Then she thought of the time after this night. Days when she would have to work side by side with this man. Nights when as an employee she would have to witness the sight of her successor beside him at Abbaye, for whatever he said now, in the cold light of morning she was sure it would be different. She thought of the unknown Ginny who had been dying to spend this very weekend in Con's bed and she thought of how she would feel when it was her turn to be discarded.

'I can't—I'm sorry. I don't want to go any further.' She pulled back and he came to a shivering stop, holding her very still, eyes closed as if a physical pain had struck him.

'Kimmy, why not?' he breathed, scarcely giving her time to answer. 'Don't you trust me?'

'How can I, after what you said?' she asked brokenly, knowing by the way he held her that he was going to let her go. 'There's too much against you to let me trust you.' She meant Ginny, but she couldn't mention having seen the card with its private message, and Con misunderstood.

'Why should something from the past affect us now? We have to live for the present and the future. The past is done with. I'm sorry your mother was upset when she lost the house and that you were given in custody to your father when you'd rather have been with her, and I can understand how bitter you must be feeling. It wouldn't happen now— things have changed. But, regrettable though all that is, the past can't be altered. It's over. What matters is the here and now.'

Kim's face paled in the moonlight, her eyes darkening in pain. 'You don't see it, do you? You simply don't see what you all did to her.' Her face froze with the agony of shattered illusions. His heart really must be made of stone as she had originally surmised, for how else could he bring himself to say such a thing, wiping out the past, its lives, its hopes and loves, with one callous remark like that?

'Leave me alone, Con Arlington. This is no good. I don't want to speak to you ever again. Please leave me!'

Turning out of his arms, she groped her way along the dark path, blindly stumbling back in the

direction of the house. A group of revellers caught
sight of her and, thinking she was alone, swept her
up with them, bearing her off towards the dancing
that had spilled out on to the lawns. One swift look
over her shoulder revealed Con, face white in the
surrounding darkness, staring after her.

He stood for what seemed like an age. Then, not
being the sort of man to brood alone in an empty
garden, he rejoined the party, sweeping up the first
unattached female he saw and diving into the thick
of the dancing crowd with her.

Kim escaped her own group when a call from the
balcony showed her Con's uncle David beckoning
to her.

She made her way up to his vantage point, a white
bloom in her hand, her only birthday offering.

'Con didn't tell me it was your birthday,' she
explained.

'My dear, it's more than enough for an old has-
been like me to have a lovely young woman like
you beside me! Come, sit here and tell me why you
and my nephew are not gazing into each other's
eyes.'

'Probably because he's gazing into someone
else's,' she remarked bitterly, taking a seat on the
empty couch on the balcony and trying not to focus
too much on the red shirt and black hair of Con
Arlington in the thick of the crowd down below.

'Have you told him you love him?'

She shook her head, unsurprised that he should
come straight to the point. She had noticed his eyes

weighing the glances she and Con exchanged. 'It's more complicated than that,' she admitted. Then she told him about the block lying between them—how over the years the name Arlington-Forbes had come to mean everything callous and destructive and how Con didn't seem to care about the tragedy that had sprung from his actions, and when the old man raised his head in puzzlement, she explained how, through Con's cleverness in court all those years ago, he had stripped her mother and herself of their only possession, East Leigh.

'Mother grew up there. It was a house that had been in her family for four generations. The gardens were something she lived for—her paintings were all of the famous East Leigh rose gardens. Then Father made it impossible for her to go on living in the house. He moved into a separate wing and gradually installed a succession of girlfriends. Mother began to spend more and more time painting in Cornwall. I was away at school. Then he started to tell everyone she was unfit to have custody of a ten-year-old. He tried to make them believe she was wildly promiscuous.'

'And was she?'

Kim looked startled. 'If she was, I certainly never knew anything about it.' She paused. 'But it's true that by that time she had lovers too. She was very beautiful. She was also very loving, very caring. I can't remember ever being unhappy with her.'

'And the sun always shone,' he said gently. 'I'm sorry, my dear. Childhood often seems like para-

dise in retrospect, not that I doubt your feelings—
I mean I can understand your anguish now to discover that the man you love was instrumental in
destroying what was most beautiful in your past.
A dilemma indeed.'

He lifted his shaggy white head. 'Strange, the
English, this double standard they have. I've lived
over here long enough to regard myself as a
foreigner in this respect. Take your father: he is
allowed his women, but what is a beautiful woman
without a husband supposed to do?' He smiled.
'Myself, I can't see Conan condemning her for
having lovers! He's quite keen on things being fair
and equal!'

'This was the so-called "tug-of-love" case
anyway, well before he joined his uncle's set,' Kim
put in. 'I don't blame him for what happened then.'

'Ah yes, so we come back to Alexander Forbes.
A very different proposition.' Uncle David's tone
suggested that he didn't much care for the man.
'Conan, I believe, took over the case, much against
his will. It was regarded as something for him to
test his teeth on, the young pup. Alexander was like
that, setting up challenges along the way. He was
an exacting devil, didn't like the idea of life being
easy for anybody on his payroll. I suppose you
know he paid for Conan's education?'

Kim shook her head.

'Conan senior, his father, died when your
Conan——' he smiled, 'was just starting prep
school. Alexander took him over. His mother was

only too pleased to have her brother take over the responsibility for her son's education. And, being childless himself, Alexander wanted somebody to follow in his footsteps. Luckily Conan had always had an aptitude for the law, though I suspect the idea wasn't too popular with him to begin with. He hates being forced into anything. And I would guess he always felt Alexander was taking too much for granted.' He narrowed his eyes at her. 'You do know what happened after the case involving your parents' dispute, don't you?'

Kim shook her head. Con had his arms wrapped tightly around a frizzy-haired little piece in a white dress.

'He's been dancing beneath this balcony in full view for some minutes. I expect he'll stay there so long as you're watching,' observed the old man shrewdly. He leaned over and took her hand. 'Let me tell you something. It was because of what Conan was expected to do on behalf of your father, one of Alexander's wealthiest clients, that he resigned and joined another set, dropping also the name Forbes. You see,' he smiled, 'your family is not the only one riven by dissent.'

'So he fell out with his uncle Alexander?'

'That's putting it mildly. Can you imagine Conan "falling out" with anyone? And when I tell you that Alexander is ten times more stubborn——? Well, I'm sure you get the picture!'

'But what happened? Everyone thought he did wonderfully well in court. He made his name, so I'm told.'

'Conan has some Forbes characteristics—the best ones, I might add—but he's also a true-blue Arlington. Some things he will not do. He was young then, felt he was obliged to comply with Alexander's wishes. But he resigned as soon as the job was done. He felt he'd paid his debt to Alexander by that time.' Uncle David nodded, approving his nephew's independence. 'But you must ask him about all this yourself, my dear.'

Kim looked between the wrought-iron bars of the balcony. Con's red shirt was now nowhere to be seen. Sadly she turned to the old man. 'Thank you for telling me. I don't suppose it matters really. I would never be happy with someone like Con anyway. I guess I'm the faithful type, and when I fall in love I shall expect my husband to be faithful too.'

After a few more words about this and that she eventually made her way into the corridor outside. David was besieged by young women again, and Kim wondered if his obvious penchant for them was one of the Arlington characteristics he had been referring to with such approval.

She was just about to go downstairs when a flash of colour in the hall below caught her attention. The great chandelier was unlit, but sconces of subdued flame shed enough light to make out a figure in a red shirt in one of the doorways. It was

Con, of course. He was still with the girl in the white dress. Kim couldn't quite make out what was happening, but there was no doubt that Con had his arms round her, half carrying her, the girl's giggles coming clearly up to where Kim was still frozen on the stairs. She couldn't help watching as Con dragged the girl into one of the ante-rooms.

With a stifled exclamation she swivelled back up the stairs, and scarcely able to control her feelings flung herself into the privacy of her own room. How could he? she thought wildly. Only half an hour ago he was holding me as if I were the only woman in the world—and I was even beginning to believe him!

She gave a bitter laugh. From the start she had known he had no heart, and there had been ample proof along the way. Despite what his uncle said about the reasons for his actions in the past, there was no getting away from what he was like now. What a fool she had been to allow her opinion to be swayed by that silver tongue of his! The best thing she could do was to pack now and leave first thing in the morning.

She had half her clothes already crammed roughly into her weekend bag when the door flew open and without a word of apology Con swept into the room. When he saw what Kim was doing he strode over, coming to a halt beside her, glowering down with an expression that made her flinch. 'What the hell do you think you're doing? Planning a moonlight flit?'

'You bet!' she exploded.

'You might find transport fairly difficult to organise at this time of night.'

'I'll walk if necessary.'

He looked wildly round the room, then spying what he was after moved to the dressing-table, picking something up with an exclamation of triumph. 'Right. So let's see how far you get without this!'

Kim leapt to her feet. 'Give me back that passport!'

'Don't be stupid!'

She lunged towards him, but he held it up out of range and she could only spit and snarl like an irate kitten as he laughed softly at her useless attempts to wrest it from him. With a cold smile he slipped it inside his shirt. 'There now. If you want it you know what you can do.'

'I hate you, Con Arlington!' she burst out, tears of frustration swimming in her eyes. 'Why don't you just go back to your horrible little girlfriend? I'm sure she's missing you already.'

'If you mean the girl in the white dress, I doubt she's missing anybody. She's flat out in the blue salon and will probably stay like that until half-way through tomorrow.'

'How inconvenient for you!'

'Not in the least. Look here,' he scowled, 'can we stop arguing about other people and concentrate on ourselves? First I want to know what the hell you think you're doing. Did David say something to send you running away like this, because if so I'll break his——'

'No, he didn't,' she broke in hastily. 'In fact——' Kim hesitated, wondering whether to tell him what his uncle had passed on to her about his difference with his other uncle, but she didn't get the chance, for Con bent down, gripping her by the forearm with a strength that made her wince.

'Why are you packing, then?' he demanded fiercely. 'Don't you know this is meant to be a party?'

'I don't feel like partying, thank you. I feel like going home to sanity.'

'I doubt whether you'd find that in your home with you in it. Look, Kim,' he checked himself again, 'we always seem to go off at a tangent. Let's keep to the facts.'

'Think you're in court again, Mr Arlington? I don't want to listen to you. There's nothing you can say that I want to hear. Your uncle straightened out a few things, but nothing he can say can alter what you really are.'

'What's that?' He looked mystified.

'You're just——' She felt confused now that he was looking at her with that wide-open expression as if anything she said would be listened to and duly considered on its merits. 'You like women too much!' she blurted, turning and blushing furiously.

'Oh, that.' When she sneaked a glance at him he was looking enormously relieved. 'Well, yes, it's true. You have a point. There are some pretty ones around. But I promise never to look at another woman when we're——' He paused and for the first time she saw him look unsure. It was uncharacteristic, and the rarity of it pulled her right round.

'When we're what?' she asked, staring at him.

'Wait, not too fast! I can explain about the girl in the white dress. She had too much to drink. I thought the best thing would be to tuck her up on a couch and let her sleep it off. I didn't touch her in anything but a brotherly way—ask her when she comes round. Who else is there? Lisette, I suppose? Yes, about a year ago we had a short, as I thought, friendly affair. But she wanted to tie me up in marriage and I didn't guess until too late. She knows it's over. But she can't help flirting and hoping. Who else? Honestly, Kim,' he came to stand in front of her, 'there is no one else. I haven't wanted to look at anyone else since I met you. Since before that, actually,' he added, rather spoiling his declaration, 'because I've been working like a slave for the last six months.' He frowned. 'Anyway, why does it matter?'

Ignoring that, she gave a rueful smile. 'You're very plausible, Con. If I didn't know otherwise I would believe what you've just said. It must be the blue eyes—they give you a distinct advantage.' She wanted to cry. He really did look as if he was telling the truth. And she felt everything inside her forcing her to forgive him. But a relationship based on deceit wouldn't be worth having. 'There is someone you've forgotten, of course. There's poor, and probably by this time heartbroken, Ginny.'

There was a pause. How, she wondered, trying to be cool about it, would he talk his way out of this one?

'Ginny?' Con looked puzzled, then a smile began to light his face. 'Kim, are you really jealous? Really and positively? If you are, logic leads me to believe it can only mean one thing.'

'You're playing for time, Con. Who is she?'

He put his hands in his pockets and grinned down at her, enjoying making her wait, looking happier than she had seen him for a long time. 'Ginny, darling Ginny. She's my cousin, you precious idiot—Ginny Forbes. She's eighteen and a little devil. She knew I'd be at the Arlington clan gathering this weekend, so she talked me into letting her have my flat. For herself and a schoolfriend, she says, but I've no intention of checking up.'

He stepped forward and seemed about to pull her into his arms, but she stepped back over the pile of clothes on the floor, saying, 'I expected some elaborate excuse, nothing as simple as a cousin. Give me time.'

'Fair enough.' Con chuckled softly. 'I'll introduce you next time we're in town. You'll get on like a house on fire.' Then he frowned. 'But how in hell do you know about her?'

Kim looked shamefaced. 'I couldn't help reading her postcard the other morning. I'm sorry—I feel horrible about it.'

'That? I'm not surprised you read it. Written in red capitals! You'd have had to be blind not to. She loves teasing people. I expect the postman had a good chortle over it. Now,' he went on, frowning and turning away, 'as it seems to be question-and-answer time, I must ask you again what you meant when you accused me of murdering your mother. I assume you meant it as a metaphor?'

'It was a rather melodramatic way of putting it,' Kim admitted, stumbling over the words, knowing that what she said must affect him in one way or another. Now she knew he had resigned his position with the family law firm over what had happened, it made it difficult to explain why she had thought so badly of him.

Having heard his defence, and at long last accepting what she knew in her own heart, she could tell he was the sort of man who would be deeply affected to learn that he had caused an innocent person to suffer. She bit her lip and wondered how she could spare him.

'Kim. You're the one playing for time now. What were you really trying to say?'

'I can't—it doesn't matter now. I was talking wildly,' was the lame response. 'Drop it, will you?' She should have known a remark like that would act like a red rag to a bull.

Con stepped over the pile of clothes and dragged her against him, swivelling her hips to make her look directly into his face. 'Now I can see your expression, and it's very interesting. Do I believe what I read there?'

Kim closed her eyes.

'Open them.'

She did so.

'Now speak. I want to hear it all.'

'It's just—it's just that over the years—I thought of you as the one who——' She shook her head. 'Please, Con, it doesn't matter. I was wrong, I suppose. It's just—that's how it seemed to me then. I was only seventeen, for heaven's sake!' She tried to struggle free, but instead of letting her go he forced her over to the bed, making her sit down next to him, one arm trapping her.

'The beginning is usually a good place to start.'

'Damn you, Con, you're bullying me!'

'Very well, let's agree on that. I'm bullying you. Now, talk.'

'Do you never let anyone off the hook?' she sighed.

'Never. My reputation rests on it. Talk, I said.'

'When you did your bit in court so brilliantly and we lost East Leigh, Mother was utterly devastated,' Kim began. 'I don't know whether you know it, but as soon as I was sixteen I ran away from Dad and his latest woman friend and went to find Mother. I knew she was somewhere in Cornwall because we'd managed to keep in touch through one of her friends. I turned up at the cottage one day. It was——' she lifted her head, tears staining her cheeks, 'it was wonderful to be back with her. We had such a lot of time to make up. She'd wanted me back all those years and I knew it. And yet... and yet once we were back together we were more or less camping out in the cottage in Cornwall. I love it. We talked and we painted and we went for long walks on the cliffs, and for a few short weeks of that summer we swam and went for picnics. It was heavenly. And yet I know for her it all seemed makeshift—all she lived for was getting the courts to hand over East Leigh to me so that we would live there for good. I think she had some crazy idea of being able to recreate my childhood, so that we could relive the years denied to us.' She sighed. 'You can imagine then what a shock it was when Dad got East Leigh.'

'My doing.'

'Yes.'

'She must have hated me,' mused Con.

'Strangely enough, no. I remember the day she came back after the verdict. She refused to let me go with her—I think by then she suspected something was going to go wrong. But when she came back with the news she—she was impressed by you. ''That young Daniel'', she called you.'

'Her chap was a pretty formidable QC. I wasn't supposed to be able to run rings round him. I just did more homework than he did,' said Con.

'She knew that. On merit she saw it was right you won. But on justice—well . . .'

'I'm sorry.' His voice sounded strangely deflated.

Kim hoped he would leave it there, but she should have known better.

'You haven't yet explained why you called me murderer,' Con went on.

'No.'

'You're going to.'

'Am I?' she returned, looking suddenly stubborn.

He touched a curl below her ear. 'Please. Hold nothing back from me now.'

'No, Con, let's leave it there.'

'Kim, if you have any consideration for me, tell me the whole of it.'

'Consideration?' She gave a little smile. Then she put a hand on his shoulder. 'I was talking wildly and I know now it would be the very last thing you intended. I've been wrong to blame you, Con, for what happened, but I was so——' she gave a quick sigh, 'I wanted a scapegoat, I suppose.'

'All right, I understand that. Now tell me what happened.'

She took a deep breath, reluctant, even now, to begin. Then, not looking at him, she said, 'Two days after the verdict, Mother made out a will leaving me all her paintings and a few pieces of jewellery. All she had. And then,' Kim's knuckles shone white on her lap, 'and then—oh, no . . .' She shook her head.

'Please, Kim.'

Her eyes were huge and shiny, turned full on him as he drew the words from her. 'One day shortly afterwards she simply walked down the cliff path below the cottage and—she walked out across the beach and into the sea. And she kept on walking. Her body was washed up a few weeks later.' Tears were flowing silently down her cheeks now. 'You see,' she went on, 'I knew it was because of the court case, and yet I feel I could have stopped her because she warned me beforehand, but I didn't understand what she meant. She said, "They've finished me off, darling. I can't fight any more." East Leigh was more than just a house, you see. It was the heart of all her work. All her dreams of love and contentment were based there. Her very best work came from that time when everything was still good.'

Con took her into his arms, cradling her. He didn't kiss her, but she could feel his face against hers, becoming washed by her own tears. Her lashes were wet and she was crying for her mother, but she was crying for Con too.

When she opened her eyes she looked into his face, trying to gauge what effect her words had had. For once the blue had dulled, and his face was sombre as he held her close.

'Nothing I can say would be adequate,' he told her simply. He was silent.

'Con?'

He looked down.

'Nothing's changed.'

'Well,' he said, misunderstanding, 'you can't deny you felt something for me.'

CHAPTER TEN

CON bent down and began to fold her clothes and pack them inside the case without speaking. Before he finished he got up abruptly and went out of the room without a word. A few minutes later Kim heard one of the guests' cars roar rapidly out of the courtyard at the front of the house. There was a sound at the door and Mariette poked her head round.

'Oh, you're still here. How extraordinary! Con has just driven away in my car.' Then, seeing Kim's expression, she came hurrying in, her face full of concern. 'Have you had a quarrel, *chérie*?'

Kim nodded. It had all happened so quickly she wasn't sure whether they had or not. She tried to explain to Mariette. 'I told him I no longer blamed him for what happened, and he didn't say anything—but before I knew what he intended he'd gone!'

Mariette nodded. 'He rarely loses control. For him not to stand and argue his ground must mean he is perhaps confused.' She gave Kim a brief hug. 'Don't worry, he'll drive for an hour or so and when he comes back he will have sorted it all out in his head. Trust him.'

'I never knew love could hurt like this.' Kim went to the window and looked out. The sky was silvered over now with the sun lying just below the horizon. It would be another fine summer's day, and she longed to share it with Con.

An hour later he was still missing, and Mariette went back to her flat across the courtyard, apparently undisturbed by the fact that he was driving her car. The other guests gradually went off to their rooms or home until finally Kim seemed to be the only person awake in the whole domain. She sat by her bedroom window for a long time, her ears alert for the sound of the returning car, but by the time the garden was filling with sunlight there was still no sign.

Exhausted, she lay on the bed in her clothes, imagining all kinds of things and half expecting the sound of police sirens bringing news of a motorway smash-up, determined she would stay awake until she heard Con come back.

In fact it was the housekeeper who woke her at just after ten. 'Phone for you, *mademoiselle*.'

'For me?'

Puzzled, Kim staggered downstairs to the drawing-room, only half awake as her hand reached out to pick up the receiver.

'Kim? It's me.' There was no doubt whose voice it was. 'I've decided not to come back this weekend. If you have any feelings for me at all, please make sure you've left Abbaye by tomorrow. I'll settle up with Ian about fees and so on and I guarantee Image

Design won't lose out—I'm willing to settle for the full figure. Get someone to apologise to Mariette about her car. I hope she can manage without it today. And Kim, please do as I say. You've been right all along—it is impossible. Take care, my love. God bless.'

Before she could say anything the line went dead. For a good few minutes she could only stare at the phone as if expecting it to come alive again and Con's voice to rattle down the line in its usual fashion. He had sounded so flat, so unlike himself. Her heart cried out to him. But she had no idea where he was. She fastened the belt of her housecoat a little tighter and went along the corridor to the kitchens, where she managed to ask one of the maids if Monsieur David was awake yet.

'Never before twelve if he goes to bed at dawn!' was the reply. The maids smiled among themselves. Something in Kim's expression must have conveyed itself to them, though, for one of them said, 'Is it about Monsieur Con?'

Kim nodded.

'Don't worry, I'll go in. Come.' She took Kim by the hand as if she wasn't sure whether her English had been adequate to convey what she wanted, and together they went along the corridor to David's ground-floor room. The heavy curtains only half concealed the windows and, contrary to Kim's expectations, he was propped up against a mound of tartan pillows reading a morning paper, a pair of steel-framed spectacles perched on his nose.

The maid explained something to him and went out.

Before he could say anything Kim went over to him, her face twisting in anguish. 'It's all my fault!' she exclaimed. 'I was awake all night thinking, what if something dreadful happens to him?'

'Most unlikely, my dear. Don't fret—no doubt he's basking in the sun on some exquisite beach at this very moment.'

'No, he rang just now.' She explained what Con had said to her, adding miserably, 'What will happen if I refuse to do as he says?' She lifted green eyes to the old man, wondering if he would allow her to stay at Abbaye now Con had called off the work with Image Design.

Her fears were unfounded. 'Why not try it and see?' David Arlington suggested. 'You are most welcome as my guest, dear Kim. And if Conan suggests otherwise he'll have me to deal with. Now, have you had breakfast?'

Despite his invitation, Kim felt like an impostor as she sat out on the terrace with the one or two other guests who had risen in time for the cook's home-made croissants. Every minute she expected to see Con's dark, autocratic face swim into her line of vision, and to hear the clipped tones telling her once more that she was right and their relationship was an impossibility. But there was no sign of him all that morning. It was only at midday that another call came through. This time it was for David Arlington himself. Con, she was told a few minutes later, had rung from the airport. He was catching the next flight to London. Whether he knew Kim was still at Abbaye or not they couldn't tell her. She sat on the edge of David's couch and picked at the tartan fringe of his rug.

'I must see him. It can't end like this. I must tell him he's wrong,' she said miserably. 'But he won't listen to me, will he? I know he won't.'

'I agree he's difficult to persuade once he's made up his mind about something,' David agreed, 'So why not put yourself out of your misery and go and see him?'

'I don't even know where he'll be.' She bit her lip.

'Try his Chelsea flat. If he's not there, you can always see him in chambers on Monday morning.'

'You're so calm and sensible, David.' Kim reached across and kissed him on the cheek.

'If I can't be calm and sensible at my age, dear child, there's no hope for the world! Besides, I have great faith in my nephew,' he told her, 'he's not a complete imbecile. Only if he were would you have cause to worry!' Before she left he took her hand in his. 'For what it's worth, I should imagine Con believes you will never be able to forgive him for what happened to your mother.'

'But that's ridiculous,' she replied. 'He couldn't be more wrong. I know now he wasn't responsible for it. I've already tried to explain that I only blamed him because I was looking for a scapegoat.'

'Then tell him again, my dear.'

While she waited for Raoul to get his car out to give her a lift to the airport, she mulled over David's words. There was some comfort in them, but not much. She knew how strongly Con could hold an opinion. And he had sounded so sure over the phone that they now had no future. Obviously he blamed himself for what had happened now he knew the truth.

The flight seemed endless. Kim felt overwhelmed by the noise and bustle of the Saturday travellers, everyone intent on getting to their own destinations for the weekend as quickly as possible. She felt hot and sticky and unable to think straight. All the way over she tried to think of different lines of argument she could use to persuade Con he was wrong. But nothing seemed to make sense. If he didn't want to agree, he would find a way round anything she said. It was a relief when the plane began to drop through cloud on to the runway at last, then, after minor delays at the airport, she was being carried rapidly into central London.

David had written down Con's address for her, and by the time she was sitting in a taxi being carried along the Embankment from Victoria the piece of paper it had been written on was screwed up into a tiny ball in her hand.

With a sick feeling she saw the Georgian mansion at the end of the road, then the taxi was drawing up outside the black door with the perfect wistaria round it, and then it was disappearing down the road and she was standing by herself, wondering if, after all, she had the courage to face him, knowing that the outcome would probably be a negative one.

Up until the moment she saw the door open she almost prayed Con would be out so that the inevitable would be delayed, and she tried hard to convince herself he wouldn't be at home. Then all of a sudden the door was swinging wide and she was looking up into a familiar pair of blue eyes and Con himself was gazing down at her, no greeting, no smile of welcome, on a face that showed no sign of surprise at seeing her either.

'May I come in?' she asked when he made no move to let her past.

'Is this a good idea, Kim?'

'I think so.'

He paused and for a moment she thought he was going to tell her to go away, but after a brief hesitation he stepped back to let her through.

He was looking haggard, she thought, due, no doubt, to a night without sleep. His shirt, tiny blue and red check, was rumpled up as if he had slept in it, and he had a navy blue V-neck sweater pulled on any old how over it. His usually sleekly groomed hair was ruffled and looked as if he hadn't bothered to comb it since they had last met.

'It seems ages ago since we were in Abbaye,' she said wondering how to begin.

'A lifetime,' he agreed. He didn't ask her to sit down and he himself stood in the hall as if he didn't want her to penetrate any further into his domain—as if, having told her it was impossible, he meant to keep her out of any part of his life.

Frightened by his determination to stand by what he had told her, she felt her mouth go dry. She had to force herself to speak. 'Is Ginny here?' she asked, hoping for some ordinary explanation like that for his refusal to invite her into the sitting-room.

He shook his head. 'They've gone out.'

'I see.' Kim stared and stared, at a loss for words, all the words of persuasion, of forgiveness, of love, failing her at the crucial moment, until she took a grip on herself and, calm enough to surprise herself, repeated the words she had said when they last met.

'Nothing has changed for me, Con.'

'You mean you've come all this way to tell me that?' His voice was hoarse.

'I had to. I don't want us to part with any misunderstandings between us.'

'We haven't. Everything is now more than clear.' He paused. 'I don't blame you. In fact I thoroughly understand your point of view. I would feel exactly the same way myself in your circumstances. I would hate me too.' He gave a bitter smile. 'Don't feel guilty about that.' He moved towards the door. 'Nothing I can say will ever convey how I feel at this moment. Now, please, leave me, Kim. I—I don't wish to continue what can only be a rather futile exchange.'

'Con, I don't think you really heard me. I said nothing's changed. I mean, nothing's changed from the moment I understood what I felt about you.'

He was stopped on the verge of saying something else, she could tell by the slight double-take he made, and he eyed her with caution before giving a small, knowing smile, saying, 'Of course. And it's been all hate, hasn't it? You made that quite clear. It's just that I was pigheaded enough not to want to believe you. I thought I could talk you into changing your mind. I've already said I don't blame you. My attentions must have been utterly repugnant to you. I'm so sorry, Kim. Pain is the last thing I want to cause anyone, least of all you. I would rather suffer myself ten thousand times than have you hurt in any way.'

She moved rapidly across the intervening space, putting a hand up to his face. 'Stop it, Con! Listen to me. You said in Abbaye I couldn't deny I felt something for you, and I said you're quite right. Now you're looking at me as if I'm twisting the words to mean their opposite.' She almost smiled. 'That's what *you* would do.'

'And?'

'And I'm not doing that, Con. I'm not twisting anything. I'm agreeing with you, heaven help me.' She slipped her arms around his neck, not caring any longer if he pushed her away, longing only to feel him close again. It was like being at home to feel his familiar shape against her, and his arms slid round her waist, holding her lightly as if he wasn't sure she meant him to hold her at all.

'Can't you tell I feel something, Con?' she whispered against the side of his neck. Her head tilted.

He looked down at her flushed face and parted lips, and his hands began to caress her despite his apparent lack of volition in the matter, and he admitted, 'I can only say, you'd never get away with a flat denial. So what's the catch?'

'The catch is—I love you. I can't help it. And I doubt whether even you could talk me out of it.'

'Would I try?' he asked. His expression changed. His eyes began to live again. Locking her feverishly in his arms, he said again, 'Would I ever try?'

'But there is something,' she whispered.

'Yes?'

'You have to tell me something about the case. Why you left Forbes-Arlington straight afterwards.'

'Mind your own business.' He began to press hot kisses on to her face, but she pushed him away.

'Listen to me, Con. When we talked in Abbaye-sur-Lac you told me it was question-and-answer time. You said we must hold nothing back from each other.'

'Don't throw my words back at me!' he sighed.

'If I can't, who can?'

Con let his arms drop abruptly from around her waist and paced over to a window. It reminded Kim of the previous night when they had started to talk and then things had gone so disastrously wrong.

Then the night had still been alive with the sound of dance music. The moon hung in a corner of her bedroom window. Now Con, his back to her, was outlined against the reds and blues of stained glass and sunlight flooded through.

He took his time to give her an answer and when he did he spoke carefully. 'My reasons were my own then, and they still are. I had enough of all this at the time. David has evidently given you the gist of what happened all that time ago. Alexander liked things his own way. We disagreed on general policy. I thought it best to get out while I still had a reputation worth having.'

'That's all probably true. But is it the whole truth?'

'Why should you think otherwise?' He turned.

Kim kept very still. Hardly daring to utter the words, she said, 'Even though you didn't know the full repercussions from what you once called the Flaxton-Wetherby case I think the result may have influenced your decision to leave Forbes.'

'So what if it did?' he almost barked. 'It doesn't alter the stark fact that I was instrumental in causing your mother's death.' Suddenly he was beside her. 'Listen to me, Kim, I don't want you to get any false ideas about me. What I did when the case was over and why I did it has no relevance. I was young, I was an idealist. Forget it. Don't go making anything of it. I knew I was in a very strong position, career-wise. I was young, and I'd made a splash. I could make my own rules. But Alexander tried to stop me, and I was determined I wasn't going to kowtow to him or anyone else. I didn't care a damn about anybody.'

'Including your wealthy clients?'

He caught her glance and smiled grudgingly, 'OK, including my wealthy clients.'

'You make yourself sound quite nasty,' she remarked as mildly as she could while burningly conscious of a need to be in his arms. 'Please may we sit down in your sitting-room?' she asked in a small voice.

He gave a shrug and his lips twisted. 'You don't give up easily, do you?'

'Don't you think it's good that we have some traits in common?'

He didn't answer, but instead led her through into the next room and pushed her down beside him on the chesterfield. She felt his muscular weight crushing against her.

'Listen to me, Kim. I was bloody ruthless in those days. I knew if I didn't get out pretty quick I'd be swallowed up by the Forbes gang. I was egotistical enough to want to hear my own name on everybody's lips.'

'Very nasty,' she remarked again.

'To learn that I inadvertently drove someone to despair makes me feel——'

'Don't! You could never have guessed what would happen. Mother had a history of depression. It was not your fault, Con. She certainly never blamed you—she rather admired you. We did talk about all this, you know. And for quite a time I felt I was to blame too. But her doctor told me something that—well, she'd been depressed about her health too. When I accused you of—I was so confused when I met you, I wanted to blame someone. And over the years it had been easy to blame someone I'd never met and knew nothing about. In my heart I knew you were right when you said you were doing your job. You were right, Con. Mother herself accepted that.'

'You don't know what I was like in the old days,' he apologised. 'I was ruthlessly ambitious.' His lips brushed her forehead.

'You sound nastier and nastier,' she remarked as he began to lower her gently against a pile of cushions.

'I can be even nastier if you'll let me,' he told her, his voice thickening with sudden desire.

'Show me, Con. I don't think I believe you!'

'Is this nasty enough for you?' He rapidly unfastened the ribbons that kept the front of her blouse together and slipping one hand inside ran a burning finger over her naked breasts. Then, before she could reply, her skirt rode up as he lifted her legs on to the sofa and sank down on top of her. Kim shivered with pleasure as at long last she felt the caresses she had yearned for and his voice, teasing now, murmured in her ear again and again, 'Is this nasty enough, my angel? And this? And this?'

And she whispered no to each greater intimacy as he drove her desire to the ultimate, feeling that to urge him on to dare more, to take her completely, would be the final seal on the past. And at last, when there was no holding back, she gave herself with a cry of love that confirmed for him what had been in her heart all along, and Con knew that the guilt that had lacerated him over the last few hours had been an illusion and that his ice-maiden was at last revealed as a fiery creature of true love.

By the time Ginny and her boyfriend returned to the flat, Con had booked two flights back to Abbaye for that evening. 'Ian will let you have the week off.' He came off the phone. 'I insisted you start work at once,' he told Kim.

'But what about your court case? Don't you have to be back? I shall miss you if——'

'I do wish you'd read the papers sometimes,' he scolded. 'Didn't you know we won? I'm taking a well-earned rest.'

'I'll read them every day from now on,' she told him fondly, 'especially when you're in them.'

It was evening when they arrived back at Abbaye-sur-Lac. Kim felt a slight sense of *déjà-vu* when she saw revellers dancing in the garden.

'Last night was for friends and business associates. Tonight it's strictly family.'

'Last night, or this morning?' she murmured after the introductions and they had made an excuse to go upstairs to freshen up after the flight.

Seeing the made-up bed Con looked at it longingly. 'Do you feel sleepy, angel?'

'I've forgotten how to sleep—it's so long since I did it,' she told him. 'And I'm not even going to try until I've sorted one or two things out.' She turned to him, whispering words that told as much of her love for him as any commonplace words of endearment as he held her in his arms.

'Con, now you know nothing hangs on your answer, will you tell me something. You did leave Forbes because of Mother, didn't you?'

'You know I did,' he assented gruffly when it was obvious she was going to insist on an answer. 'It sickened me—rich men clubbing together to grind one poor woman into the dust. Of course, I'd no idea she would take it as badly as she did. I thought she would pick up the pieces—marry some rich fellow, perhaps, and all would be well.'

Kim snuggled against him as he pulled her down beside him, trembling as he ran a hand down her silky length. 'Men always assume women can solve their problems by marriage.'

'What about you?' He looked down at her where she lay in the crook of his arm. 'Perhaps you've got a few problems that can be solved in that way.'

'I'm not thinking of marriage, am I?'

'I wish you would.'

He kissed her hotly all over her face and she shivered with the expectation of what it might mean, but instead of loving her he said, 'Let's finish getting changed and make ourselves look presentable.'

'What? Now?'

'No time like the present.'

'But whatever for?'

'Don't argue.' He dragged her up and with only a brief delay to kiss her breasts and take her tenderly into his arms when she was half dressed, he led her out into the corridor. He smiled for a minute as she blinked in the soft light on the landing. Then leading her along the corridor he knocked lightly on his uncle's balcony room. The old man, as spry as ever, had three or four girls petting him as he watched the fireworks someone was letting off down below.

He smiled with pleasure at the sight of Kim's happy face. Then he held out his hand. 'I suppose you want your mother's ring?' he addressed Con.

'May I?'

'I thought you'd never get around to it. Here, you young devil, let's see you put it on her finger.'

Kim was overwhelmed as the opal she had noticed when she first met David Arlington was removed from his bony old finger and Con, holding it up for a moment so that everyone could see it catch the light, slowly and solemnly placed it on her engagement finger.

Then he led her to the balcony, and as the fireworks faded in a cloud of multi-coloured stars in the darkness he called out to the people below.

Kim looked down at the pale fire of the ring on her finger for confirmation that it wasn't all a dream, then there was champagne, and the Arlingtons, one by one, welcomed her into the family and she was turning to him at last, eyes as bright as stars themselves. 'I didn't know you had so many cousins, Con, and I surely must be dreaming this. Darling Con, please tell me it's all real.'

'I'll tell you something else.' He led her away to a secluded corner. 'I heard the other day that East Leigh was coming up for sale. If you want it, I'd like to give it to you as a wedding present.' He gave her a careful look.

She removed his doubts at once. 'It would be the most perfect present you could ever give me, Con. Mother would have been so happy to know it was back in the family at last.'

He started to lead her towards the door. 'Now, everybody's heard the announcement, and even though you said you weren't thinking of marriage you're going to have to say yes.'

'Oh, Con!' She was draped in his arms again. 'You're so nasty you'd probably sue me for breach of promise if I disagreed.'

'You bet I would.' He kissed her fondly. 'You know how nasty I am.'

'Be as nasty as you like,' she whispered back, 'so long as it's going to be forever.'

'There is one more thing,' he said as they made their way not, to her surprise, to her room nor even into his across the corridor, but to a room at the far end of the house where the builders had only just finished work. 'I promised you something.'

'What was that?' she asked in astonishment, thinking that now, surely, she had everything she could ever wish for.

'So long ago it seems like another life I promised we'd dine like royalty in an orgy of pleasure.' He glanced down at the black bodice with its flounced skirt. Seeing his glance and remembering his words, she guessed what he was thinking, and she stood on tiptoe, giving him a brief warm kiss before slipping out of his arms and running back along the corridor to her room.

When she emerged a few seconds later the black dress had been discarded. In its place was the white lace confection that Con had described as a scrap of heaven.

'And you promised me a four-poster,' she teased as he opened the door into the room.

Then she gasped, for he had kept his promise. Resplendent with heavy drapes of green and gold was a bed fit for the Sun King himself. Slowly, so slowly that time seemed to stand still, Con led her over to it, pressing her down amongst its enormous pillows, muttering huskily against the side of her neck. 'I'm not feeling particularly hungry, but if you are——'

'No, I'm not,' she interrupted hastily, 'not for food, anyway. Hungry for you, ravenous, insatiably hungry for you, darling.'

And not wanting to waste a precious moment, she pulled him down to her, twisting beneath him so that he could tear away the dress that had so taunted him before. Gently he began to ease the white cotton lace up her legs, bunching it around her thighs, being careful not to snag it on the opal ring, until with a hurried twist she brought herself passionately against his hard body, crying, 'Hurry, darling! It doesn't matter about being careful. Honestly, Con, Lizzie said she wanted me to treat it roughly. To see what it would stand up to.'

'And are you going to tell her?' he asked, forgetting his caution in a wild swooping of possession as he heard what she said.

'I won't need to. She knew long before I did that I was in love with you. She told me to think about it. I wish I had.'

'Thinking time is over now anyway,' he told her. 'It's loving time for all time—and don't ever forget it!'

Harlequin Presents®

Coming Next Month

1263   A BITTER HOMECOMING Robyn Donald
Alexa returns home to find that Leon Venetos believes all the scandal broadcast about her And he wastes no time showing his contempt in unfair treatment of her Yet Alexa can't fight the attraction that binds them together

1264   WILD PASSAGE Vanessa Grant
Neil Turner, looking for crew for his boat, signs on Serena. He has no idea that, although she's lived with sailing for years, it's only been in her dreams. He soon finds out as they start down the west coast of the United States that her practical experience is actually nil!

1265   EQUAL OPPORTUNITIES Penny Jordan
Sheer desperation leads Kate Oakley to employ a man as nanny for nine-month-old Michael, her friend's orphaned baby. And while Rick Evans comes with impeccable references, he has his own motives for wanting to be in her life.

1266   WITH NO RESERVATIONS Leigh Michaels
Faced with running the old family hotel, Lacey Clinton soon realizes she isn't properly qualified to restore it. Selling to rival hotelier Damon Kendrick seems the answer—until she learns he doesn't want the hotel unless Lacey comes with it.

1267   DREAMS ON FIRE Kathleen O'Brien
Megan Farrell already dreads locking horns with the new owner of the New Orleans rare book shop where she works. But even she has no idea how easily this man can destroy her firm ideas about the past—and especially those about love and passion.

1268   DANCE TO MY TUNE Lilian Peake
Jan accepts as just another job the assignment of tracking down Rik Steele and reconciling him and his father. When she falls in love with her quarry, she has a hard time convincing him that she's not just interested in the money.

1269   LEAP IN THE DARK Kate Walker
When a stranger kidnaps Ginny and the two children she's temporarily looking after, Ginny doesn't know where to turn for comfort. All her instincts tell her to turn to Ross Hamilton—but he's the man holding them captive.

1270   DO YOU REMEMBER BABYLON Anne Weale
Singer Adam Rocquaine, idolized the world over, can have any woman he wants. And it seems he wants Maggie. She knows a brief fling in the public eye would leave her miserable—yet she wonders if she has the strength to say no.

Available in May wherever paperback books are sold, or through Harlequin Reader Service:

In the U.S.
901 Fuhrmann Blvd.
P.O. Box 1397
Buffalo, N.Y. 14240-1397

In Canada
P.O. Box 603
Fort Erie, Ontario
L2A 5X3

**In April, Harlequin brings you the
world's most popular romance author**

JANET DAILEY

No Quarter Asked

Out of print since 1974!

After the tragic death of her father, Stacy's world is shattered. She needs to get away by herself to sort things out. She leaves behind her boyfriend, Carter Price, who wants to marry her. However, as soon as she arrives at her rented cabin in Texas, Cord Harris, owner of a large ranch, seems determined to get her to leave. When Stacy has a fall and is injured, Cord reluctantly takes her to his own ranch. Unknown to Stacy, Carter's father has written to Cord and asked him to keep an eye on Stacy and try to convince her to return home. After a few weeks there, in spite of Cord's hateful treatment that involves her working as a ranch hand and the return of Lydia, his ex-fiancée, by the time Carter comes to escort her back, Stacy knows that she is in love with Cord and doesn't want to go.

**Watch for *Fiesta San Antonio* in July and
For Bitter or Worse in September.**

Have You Ever Wondered If You Could Write A Harlequin Novel?

Here's great news—Harlequin is offering a series of cassette tapes to help you do just that. Written by Harlequin editors, these tapes give practical advice on how to make your characters—and your story— come alive. There's a tape for each contemporary romance series Harlequin publishes.

Mail order only

All sales final
